Ellie White

GW00503256

A

Romance

For

Christmas

By Ellie White

ISBN: 9798865676089

Imprint: E White Publishing

Editing: Aimee Walker

Cover Design: Ellie White - Image Copyright Purchased from Shutterstock

Also by Ellie White

Standalone Novels

Love & London

Love in the Wings

A Wearside Story

Book 0.5 - Playing For You (A Wearside Story Novella)

Book 1 - Playing For Her

Book 2 - Playing For Real - April 2024

Romance Redefined - Novellas

A Romance For Christmas

The Romance Retreat - July 2024

A Romance For Christmas

This is for the Christmas Hallmark movie lovers who wish there was added spice!

A Romance For Christmas

Chapter One

Zara

The room is filled with writhing bodies making all sorts of peculiar noises.

Moans, slapping flesh and cries of ecstasy to name a few.

Not to mention the Christmas songs the DJ insists on playing. It is a Christmas party I suppose. Just not the kind of Christmas party I'm used to.

I can't believe I actually thought this would be a good idea.

Me... Zara McIntosh. Chronic good girl, people pleaser and rule follower. Married my high school sweetheart at eighteen to please my parents and form one of the most connected and influential families in the North East of England. I spent a decade pleasing my husband too. Or at least I thought I was. He never complained once about the kind of wife I was.

Ugh no, get it together Zara.

I'm here for a reason and thinking about him is not it. I can do this. I can totally do this!

A woman dressed in a long black trench coat, carrying what looks to be a riding crop, walks past me, leading a man on all fours around the room, parading him like a prized pooch at Crufts.

Oh fuck, I can't do this.

An empty seat is hidden in the shadows of a potted plant over in the corner of the already dimly lit bar, so I make my way over there as Mariah Carey's "All I Want for Christmas Is You" reaches its crescendo. The song isn't the only thing letting out high-pitched cries.

Shrugging my leather jacket from my shoulders, I reveal the black lace corset lingerie I'm trying to pass off as a top. I'm quite sure you can see my nipples through the sheer fabric, but for the first time in a long time, I felt sexy when I put it on. Like someone might actually hit on me tonight.

Fucking hell. What's wrong with me? Why did I think I belonged in a sex club for fuck's sake?

I've been touched by one man in my entire life; missionary in the dark with my husband is all I know.

Ex-husband.

Six months since I found him in a compromising position with my assistant and I still forget the "ex" in ex-husband. Probably because despite our legal divorce happening any day now, I'm still pretending to be married to him… "for his political image".

I hate how that sounds when I say it out loud. God forbid his constituents find out how much of a twat he is. Multiple women over the course of our marriage and I didn't have a clue until I caught him in the act myself.

So fucking naive.

"Hey, gorgeous. Want to have some fun?"

The husky voice belongs to an incredibly attractive man

with sandy blond hair and muscles I didn't even know existed. I recognise him from the tour I took when I first arrived, but he looks different now. The thing that strikes me as odd is that he's not dressed as festively as the others in here and closer inspection tells me he's cosplaying Thor. Well, I think that's a dildo shaped like Mjolnir, Thor's hammer, but it's so dimly lit in here it's hard to be sure.

His eyes smoulder as he checks me out and as much as I'm sure he could show me a good time tonight, I can't bring myself to say yes.

"Oh." I laugh nervously, regretting all my choices that brought me here. "I think I'm just going to watch."

He smiles. "I can put on a show for you if you'd like?"

I'm sure it'd be a great show but even this stresses me out.

"Actually, I'm… I'm parched…" I point my thumb back over my shoulder. "I'm going to the bar. Next time though for sure!"

"Ask for Stacey." His smile turns softer, friendly, as though he can sense my discomfort. "If you're nervous or unsure whether you want to do this, she's an excellent listener and makes a great Long Island iced tea."

"Is it that obvious I'm not cut out for this?" I ask.

Christ, I've never felt so embarrassed and insecure in all my life.

"A little, but we were all new here once."

"Thank you," I say.

9

As quickly as he dropped his bravado, he picks it back up again and wanders the room some more.

When I glance around the club again, it's not as scary as I first thought. The music is low and seductive with a random burst of slowed-down festive tunes. The atmosphere is sexy, and everyone is having fun in a safe and comfortable environment.

God, I wish I could be one of them. I wish I could be as carefree as they are.

But maybe that's too much to ask.

I make my way through the crowded room towards the bar, observing people cosplaying as sexy Santa, elves and even a few reindeer as I go. I guess there was a dress-up option to the party I wasn't aware of.

"I'm looking for Stacey," I say, hopping up on a bar stool. The bartender smiles softly in recognition. She's beautiful with wild blonde curls pulled up into a messy ponytail on top of her head. They bounce around as she talks.

"Simon sent you?"

"Dressed like Thor?" I guess, I never did get his name, and she nods. "Yeah, he did."

"What can I get for you, hun?"

"Long Island iced tea, please."

"Coming right up."

When Stacey turns away, I take the opportunity to look around the room in more detail from the safety of my seat. There's a guy eating a girl out on a table no more than six feet away from me and another couple tangled up like pretzels, grinding in rhythm to the drum and bass pumping through the speakers as a woman watches and touches herself.

It's hot, really hot. But still, I feel...nothing.

Absolutely, not a thing.

Shouldn't I be a little bit turned on? Is there something wrong with me?

"So, first time?" Stacey asks, saving me from going down a rabbit hole of self-exploration I'm really not ready to venture down. She slides the cold glass towards me, and I gladly take it from her, savouring that first sip. She's wearing silver tinsel shaped into a halo above her head that I didn't notice at first. Angel Gabriel, eat your heart out.

"Yeah, I thought... Well, I don't know what I thought..." Although my words make no sense whatsoever, she seems to understand.

"It's okay to be nervous or unsure."

I glance back at the girl on the table who is definitely having a much better time here than I am.

"I mean, this is great... She's gorgeous, he's gorgeous. He looks like he knows what he's doing, and she's loving it. But I don't feel anything. I don't feel like I want to get involved or you know...do stuff myself." I sigh audibly, taking another long, delicious gulp through my straw.

To be fair to this place, this is the best Long Island iced tea I've ever tasted.

"What made you come here in the first place?"

Stacey, which I suspect is more of a code name than her actual name, is a stranger, but something about her reassures me that I'm safe. Like a therapist that cost me three hundred pounds entry fee to see.

"I've always been curious about sex, but my family is religious so it was always taboo. And my husband, ex-husband, didn't really want to experiment and explore until he met his mistress. I thought here, I could experience great sex without that emotional connection."

"Some of us thrive in this environment, but others need safety and comfort in order to really open themselves up. Having an emotional connection with someone isn't a terrible thing. When you find the right person, it comes naturally."

She's right. I know she is. So why do I feel like a failure?

"Do you have a phone I could use? They made me check mine in and I don't want to wait outside for a taxi."

Tonight has been a bust, and all I want now is to go home to my own bed and watch crappy TV until I pass out.

"Here." Stacey hands me a cordless phone from behind the bar with pity in her eyes. "Don't call a taxi, call a friend."

I contemplate calling my brother to pick me up, but how would I explain this to him without outing my failed marriage and shattering the perfect picture he has of me?

There's no other choice. I dial the only other phone number I sort of, vaguely, remember from my childhood and hope to god he picks up.

Chapter Two

Noah

"Still no girlfriend, son?" my dad asks for the third time this afternoon as we sit around the Christmas tree in the conservatory of his care home. The old-fashioned wireless plays calming festive melodies and we snack on mini slices of Christmas cake I brought in. I've never been a fan of traditional cake, but I eat it anyway.

Christmas was always Dad's favourite time of year; it still is now even though he's slowly drifting away from me. He would always make a big deal of it when I was a kid, taking me to see Santa, and joining in with the carollers that gathered on the village bandstand on Christmas Eve.

Every year, we'd make a Christmas cake together. I suppose I still make it now out of habit.

"No, Dad. Still no girlfriend," I say with a shrug.

"You better hurry up, son. I don't want you to be alone forever. Some of my best memories are with your mam."

A dark shadow crosses his face as he struggles to process his thoughts and my heart plummets to my stomach. It's always the same when he mentions her, as though he's trying to remember what happened and why she doesn't visit him too.

My parents had me when they were in their forties. For Dad, I was the thing he never realised he needed in his life until I arrived. For Mam, I was the result of one too many wines and missed birth control. She tried her best after I was born, but she never wanted kids; I wasn't part of her plan.

Dad was heartbroken when she eventually left us. I was two years old, so I don't have any memories of my own but Dad did. They'd been married for a long time before I was born, and he struggled knowing she didn't love him enough to stay and work through it.

"Dad, are you okay?" I ask, though there's no coming back now. It's always the same result when he gets that vacant look in his eyes. The once strong and dependable man I grew up admiring is now an aged shadow of himself, so small and frail.

Dad started displaying signs of Alzheimer's disease a few years ago. It started with him forgetting the little things, like where he put his car keys or the names of people he knew. He quickly deteriorated to the point he couldn't be left alone.

A little over a year after his diagnosis, he started forgetting me and I had no choice but to move him into an assisted living complex. The best money could buy in our county. It's the least I can do after all he's given me.

A switch flips and so begins the downward spiral.

"Where am I?" Dad's frantic eyes search the room as panic builds, the setting now unfamiliar to him. "Where am I?! Who are you?! Meredith! Meredith!" he calls out for Mam with deep desperation.

"Dad, Dad, please. It's me. Noah. Mam…she's not here," I tell him as my heart shatters into a million pieces, the same way it always does when he forgets me.

"No! Meredith! Where is she? Where is my wife?"

"She's not here, Dad. I'm sorry."

I'm jostled out of the way by two nurses who dash in to attempt to calm him down. He's crying uncontrollably as confusion takes hold of him. He has no idea what's going on and he's scared.

It kills me, helplessly standing with my back pressed against the wall, and all the while, the happy Christmas music continues to play as though my emotions aren't crumbling.

I hate this feeling more than anything in the world. I hate seeing him like this, so broken and confused.

I hate that after having only each other for thirty-two years I'm not enough to keep him safe and protected.

I hate leaving him, not knowing what state I'll find him in next time. But I have to, because it's what's best for him.

"I'll call you once he's settled and in bed," the head nurse tells me as she comes to escort me out of the home. She's been here since his first day and often takes on this caring role of a matriarch of the facility. She places her soft ageing hand on my arm. "This isn't your fault, Noah."

Guilt rises up my throat like bile. It feels like it's my fault.

I give her a tight smile and nod, desperate to keep my emotions inside. I don't want anyone to see me fall apart. When I reach the safety of my truck, I pull out my phone and dial Jackson, my best friend. I don't know what I plan to say but after a few rings, it clicks to voicemail anyway. It's no surprise. Since he started dating Dutch socialite Nikole Van Blair six months ago, he's been preoccupied to say the least.

My truck purrs to life and without pause I pull out of the care home car park, doing my best not to glance in my rear-view mirror where I'll likely get a view of Dad sitting in the conservatory window looking out helplessly as I drive away from him.

As a kid, I loved Christmas; I'd count the days until Santa came. But now, I count the days until it's over.

The house phone hasn't rung in forever, so when the shrill ringing wakes me up from a restless nap on the sofa a few hours later, I dart out of my position on the couch on high alert.

The only reason the phone is still connected is because I need it for the Wi-Fi. Although, I doubt I even need it for that anymore; it's sheer laziness that I haven't disconnected it. That and the fact I haven't changed anything in this house since Dad moved out.

I haven't even decorated for Christmas the past few years, there's been no need.

Does anyone I know even have the house number? I don't even have the number. And yet, something in my gut tells me to answer it.

"Hello?"

Heavy music sounds from the other end among other

strange noises I can't quite make out. Was that someone moaning? Is this a prank call? Or a butt dial that I really don't want to continue listening to? I'm about to hang up when a small voice speaks up, struggling to be heard.

"Noah? Please tell me I got the right number this time?"

"Zara?"

Zara McIntosh. My best friend's little sister.

Emotion sparks in my chest at the sound of her voice. Emotion I really need to get under control.

Zara is six years younger than Jackson and me, and I suppose I've always been protective of her, but lately, that protectiveness seems to have morphed into something else entirely. Something I definitely shouldn't be feeling about my best friend's little sister. Not to mention the fact she's happily married to one of the most prominent politicians of our generation.

I grit my teeth at the thought of him. She could do so much better.

"Oh, thank god! I've rung like four other people trying to remember this number!" Her voice is light and giggly. Has she been drinking? It's hard to make anything out since the bar she's in is playing such loud music, but I know enough to know this isn't normal Zara behaviour.

"Are you okay?" I raise my voice so she can hear me. I can't remember the last time she called this number, so to say this is concerning is an understatement.

"No...well, yeah, I'm fine...but I need you to pick me up."

"Okay, where?"

It comes with the territory of being a best friend, looking out for Zara.

She needs help burying a body, I'll bring a spade.

She needs bailing out of jail, I'll be there no questions asked.

Obviously neither of those options would ever be possible with her.

"I'm at Chateau Minx."

I'm stunned into silence. I have to have heard wrong.

Everyone knows she's a good girl with an image to protect, it comes with the territory when you marry a public figure. If anyone finds out she's there, the opposition will publicly crucify her and her husband.

Zara is his publicist too; she knows the risks more than anyone.

What the actual fuck is she thinking?

"I'm sorry... did you say Chateau Minx?"

"Yes!" she yells, and the background noises I couldn't discern earlier make so much more sense now.

Fuck.

I run my hand over my tired face. It shouldn't take too long to get there, but still longer than I'd like to leave her there alone.

"I'll be there in half an hour. Sit tight, okay? And be safe."

Chapter Three

Zara

"How are we doing over here?" Thor asks, or to use his other name, which I also suspect is fake, Simon.

"I called a friend and he's coming to pick me up," I tell him, draining the last of my cocktail and asking Stacey for another. They really are delicious, and if I'm going to face Noah and not be embarrassed, I'll need all the Dutch courage I can get.

"A friend?"

"Yeah, sort of. He's my brother's best friend." My new friends exchange an excited look as my fresh drink appears in front of me.

"This just got interesting," Stacey coos, leaning over the bar and propping up her chin in her hands. "Tell us about your brother's best friend. Is he hot? Single?"

Taking another long drink, I'm well and truly on my way to tipsy and my lips are feeling loose.

"Noah Williams." I sigh wistfully. "What can I say about Noah? He's gorgeous, smart, creative... and definitely fuckable. I think he's single, I've never seen him bring a girl to any of our parties or anything…"

These people are strangers, but surely since I signed an NDA coming in here, I can trust them to keep my secrets too, right?

"I sense a *but* coming," Simon says.

"There's always a *but*," Stacey agrees.

"He was my first crush. When I was fifteen, I asked him to kiss me, and he turned me down. That was my first experience of heartbreak. Of course, he didn't realise it, and I never told anyone else about that day so it's a secret I've carried with me ever since. A week after I humiliated myself, I met the man I'd later marry and so I put that crush to bed."

I wonder how different my life would have been had Noah said yes that day.

Would I still have married Colin?

Yes. Because I was always meant to marry him. It was a sound business opportunity to unite our families and my parents saw to it as soon as the opportunity to get us together arose.

"Yet here you are, some fifteen years later, still crushing on Noah. Are you telling me you've never thought of him when you're…you know…alone?"

Every single night since my separation and the odd night when I was still married, but that titbit I keep to myself, surely that makes me as terrible as my ex-husband.

"Thirteen…" I defend it as if it makes it any less pathetic. I down the last of my cocktail, shaking my head when Stacey asks if I want another. "Thirteen years."

"I don't think it's pathetic at all. You called him and he

didn't think twice before agreeing to come up here," she says. "Maybe your feelings aren't just one-sided."

"There's only one way to find out, babe," Simon says, jumping from his stool and striding away.

"He's right," Stacey agrees. "I guess we'll see how he feels when he gets here."

"You know, I think I need that third drink after all!"

***

Noah

A girl in a white lace corset and gold Lycra hot pants that barely cover her arse smiles at me when I stride up to the entrance lobby of the club. Her eyes trace the length of my body as she seductively bites her lower lip and bats her long fake eyelashes at me.

I'd be flattered by the attention on any normal night, might have even acted on it, but all I can think about is getting to Zara.

"Entry is three hundred pounds." She adds another sickly-sweet smile as though that makes the price better.

"Look, my girlfriend is in there. I'm here to pick her up. I'll be in and out in a few minutes."

I know how places like this work, they don't usually like men coming alone.

"Words like that don't impress in a place like this." She winks, smiling, despite the fact I can see she's getting annoyed at me. "Three hundred pounds please."

"Come on, please?" I'm not above begging.

"Three hundred or move aside, I have customers." Her patience wears thin. Sure enough, a queue is forming behind me of patrons waiting to enter.

"Come on, man!" a guy whines from somewhere behind me as his partner clicks her heels impatiently.

"Fine." I dig my card out of my wallet and pay the bloody entry fee. Three hundred pounds for fuck's sake. Zara better have a good explanation as to why the fuck I'm here taking her home and not her husband.

"Have a great night," the woman sings, minus her previous attitude, as I storm through the doors, pushing them open with more force than necessary.

"You're new here, right? Would you like a tour?" a helpful-looking man dressed as Thor asks.

"I'm looking for my friend. She called me from the bar phone and asked me to pick her up," I explain, trying not to let my gaze drop to the massive dildo in his hand.

"Ah, pretty little blonde thing? Perky boobs, chatty as fuck with the sweetest smile?"

"That's her." So, she's here and clearly made an impression.

"Bar is that way." He nods towards a heavy-looking wooden door. "She's right about you, you are fuckable."

"Thanks, I think."

What the fresh fuck is going on tonight?

Following his instructions, I make my way through the club. It's dark and dimly lit but I can see the lights illuminating the bar in the far corner. The place looks like Santa's sexy grotto with Mrs Claus herself bent over some contraption as an elf goes to town on her.

"Fucking Zara," I grumble to myself as I squeeze through the bodies congregating by a window where three guys, dressed as what I assume are reindeer, are putting on a hell of a show for the crowd.

When I clear through the bodies, I spot her, propping up the bar and animatedly talking to the bartender with the biggest smile on her face.

"You've got your clit pierced?" she asks loudly, and I ignore the spark that shoots to my dick at hearing her say the word clit. "Did it hurt?"

Get it the fuck together, man. She's your best mate's, married, baby sister. As if reminding myself that has ever helped before.

"Yeah, like a fucking bitch," the girl replies.

"Is it worth it?" she asks with a curious lilt.

"Ohhhh yeah…"

"Nice." Zara laughs and the girls high-five.

"Zara?"

"Noah! Oh My God!" She jumps from her stool, wrapping her arms around my neck as she dives into my arms. "You're here!"

"You called me and asked me to pick you up." She wobbles

23

as I put her down on her feet. My temper softens as she grins up at me, her eyes twinkling like they belong on that Christmas tree on the dance floor.

"Wow, you look…" Once again, this girl has left me speechless as I take her in.

Zara is dressed in a tight black miniskirt and a corset that leaves little to the imagination. She doesn't seem at all bothered that I'm staring at what I'm sure are her nipples beneath the sheer lace.

My throat bobs as I try to swallow down the lump lodged there.

For fuck's sake, I really didn't want to get a hard-on in here but seeing her like this, feeling her clinging onto my biceps and looking so bloody excited to see me, it's difficult not to be aroused by her.

I want her and I'm doing a really shit job of hiding it right now.

She lets out a soft laugh and turns on her feet, throwing on her leather jacket. "Bye, Stacey!" She grins when the bartender nods her head enthusiastically.

"Good luck, Zara!" The bartender winks in response. "And have fun."

"Where's Colin? Is he here?" I look around the room, my body tense and poised to give him hell for leaving her alone, but there are no familiar faces anywhere. There's no way he's gone into a room and left her. If he has, I'll murder him myself, never mind what will happen when Jackson finds out.

"Gone!" she says, suddenly turning away from me and

leading the way through the throng of people.

"Gone where? Did he leave you here?" I catch up to her quickly, catching her hand so I don't lose her in the crowd. She doesn't stop her determined pace until we're almost at the exit. She stops abruptly at the cloakroom as we gather our things.

"No. He's gone. Moved out! Adios, dickhead! Good fucking riddance!"

I don't have time to process the news that she and Colin have separated before she's heading straight into the street towards my truck parked at the kerb. Frost has already started to form on the pavement so when she loses her footing, I reach for her.

"Oh," she gasps as I scoop her up in my arms and walk her to my truck so she doesn't break her neck in those heels. Her arms wrap around my neck as she watches me carefully. I have a million questions for her. But I can't bring myself to ask them right now since same thing echoes in my mind over and over again.

Zara is single.

And it changes everything.

Chapter Four

Zara

The usually happy-go-lucky man with the biggest, most beautiful grin in the North East is scowling and scowling hard. I don't ever think I've seen him like this. I've certainly never seen him angry before, but this is more than that, it's... well, I don't know what this is exactly.

His heart is racing a mile a minute beneath my palm which rests on his pec and his jaw is clenched so hard I'm worried he's going to crack one of his perfect teeth.

When we reach the passenger side of his truck, not far from the club door, he places me gently onto the ground, keeping one arm wrapped around me, supporting my weight effortlessly. He opens the door for me and helps me inside.

I can see a war waging in his eyes as he leans over me and buckles my seatbelt. I'm perfectly capable of doing it myself, but I let him because, oh my god, he smells delicious.

When he's done meticulously checking I'm secure, he steps back and closes the door.

As a teenager Noah had a boyish charm about him; he was always smiling, the dimple in his left cheek popping in a way that had me swooning.

Now, he's all man with a body I know could make me feel things I've never felt before. The dimple is still there though, emphasised further when he smiles.

"I want to know everything. Tell me what he did to you," Noah demands through gritted teeth the second he climbs into the driver's side.

Huh, interesting.

"I caught him buried three-inches deep inside my assistant." I snort with laughter at my dick joke but Mr Grumpy Gills in the driver's seat is not impressed. "They were going at it on my desk in broad daylight," I explain further, taking the situation a bit more seriously this time, not an ounce of emotion in my voice. "No one can know. I haven't told anyone yet. You're the first."

"I'll fucking kill him," he growls, his temper fraying further.

It might be the sexiest thing I've seen all night; his protectiveness elicits a strong reaction from my body I haven't felt in an awfully long time, does that make me weird?

Noah is gorgeous, with his dark hair and strong jawline complete with thick black stubble and eyes so deep a shade of brown they could pass for black. He's tall and muscular, and I'm pretty sure he should have been named sexiest man on earth this year because Regé-Jean Page has nothing on him.

"I wouldn't bother. He did me a favour. I was never going to leave him despite being miserable. This gave me a reason. I was embarrassed and ashamed when I found them, but I also felt a rush of relief when I realised I didn't have to pretend anymore."

Noah doesn't say anything as he pulls away from the club, his hands gripping the steering wheel so tight his knuckles look like they're about to break through the skin.

"I was done with the mediocre conversations, the tension in the house because I wasn't a good enough wife and the absolutely terrible sex." If at all possible, his grip tightens further when I mention the word sex, so I continue, curious to see how he reacts. "You know...the kind of sex that left me so unsatisfied I had to finish myself off silently in the fucking bathroom as he snored loudly in our bed!"

After a beat, he finally speaks. "Is that what tonight's all about? You went there for better sex?"

The world outside is black as we wind through the country roads towards our village. It's a clear night. Ursa Major shines brightly in the sky and the moon illuminates the tree-lined hills in the distance. I used to hate how isolated this road between us and our neighbouring village made me feel. Especially this stretch of road where the illuminations are no longer visible.

Now, all I can think about is how wonderful being isolated from the real world would be.

"I went there to see what I've been missing my entire adult life. I'm curious and want to explore my sexuality since I've never had the chance before."

And his white knuckles are back.

"Did you find it?"

28

"If you're asking me if I hooked up tonight, the answer is no. And if you're going to judge me for going there you might as well pull over and I'll walk the rest of the way," I snap. I don't know what his problem is, but I'm not going to take it.

"I'm not judging you, Zara. This is a lot of information to take in at once." He drags his hand through his hair, keeping his eyes on the road. "I didn't expect you—"

"Of course, because Noah Williams would never see little old me as a woman with sexual needs." I wave my arms around dramatically. "You're acting like the rest of them. Are you always going to see me as some kid with a crush, Noah?"

"Don't do that." He grits his teeth and keeps his voice level. "Not now, Zara. You know I'm not like them."

"You told me I didn't know what I really wanted and that I was a kid with a crush." It's the first time I've mentioned our past with anyone, including Noah.

"You were fifteen! I'm six years older than you, Zara, of course, I didn't see you in a sexual light back then. Are you fucking insane? You *were* a kid with a crush."

"I'm not fifteen anymore." I turn my body in my seat to face him. He's still tense but now I'm wondering if it's for a different reason than I first thought. Maybe he wasn't judging me after all.

"No, you're most definitely fucking not fifteen anymore."

"What's that supposed to mean?" I probe further.

"You're going through a divorce. Now isn't the right time

for this." He sighs.

"We've been separated for six months, it's not like I've moved on overnight and decided to try visiting a sex club on a whim. I've put some serious thought into it, and I know exactly what I'm looking for. I just didn't find it there."

"What were you looking for?"

"I want to finally feel pleasure at the hands of a man and not my fucking vibrator. I want to be worshipped over and over again until I can't take it anymore. Back at the club, a guy was eating a girl out like it was his last meal. I've never had that, and I want it! I want someone to fuck me thoroughly while telling me to 'take their cock like a good girl' like it's a smutty romance novel!" The words tumble out of me, and he swerves the truck ever so slightly. "That's why I went there because I wanted to experience it in a safe and controlled space instead of some random one-nighter with a stranger. But that didn't work, so my plan needs a re-evaluation. Maybe I should try Tinder."

"No!" I hear the growl in his throat as he adjusts his pants and the vixen inside of me rejoices at the thought of him being jealous and…turned on?

"Noah?" I ask, my eyes glued to the thick ridge beneath his jeans, and I squeeze my thighs together. "What did you mean when you said I'm not fifteen anymore?"

He slams on the brakes, jerking me forward, my seat belt jarring me as we pull up outside my house. I hadn't noticed the dark fields turn into the narrow streets of our village.

"What are you really asking me, Zara?"

"Are you attracted to me?"

He lets out a long groan and runs his hands down his face before he answers the real question I wanted to ask him.

"Jackson would kill me." He watches out the window, looking for any signs of life in the neighbourhood. It's out of habit more than anything; it wouldn't be the first time a photographer camped outside my house looking to get a money shot, but thankfully tonight, all seems silent.

"Jackson would never need to find out," I argue, but he remains silent. "You're thinking about it, aren't you? You're thinking about saying that stuff to me, about doing that to me…"

I'll probably regret my alcohol-induced confidence tomorrow, but right now all I can think about it is shooting my shot with Noah for the second time.

"Of course, I'm thinking about it." He tries to adjust himself again but his jeans are too restrictive. "Shit, look at you. You're beautiful and funny and smart and so fucking annoying. It turns me on to the point of pain every time we've been in the same room for the past six months. How can I not think about it when I very clearly want you and one of the two reasons I had for staying away doesn't exist anymore?"

"Wow." His speech takes my breath away. *Six months?*

"But I can't do it, Zara. I'm sorry."

"I'm not asking for the world. I'd take a single night if I had to."

"Seriously? You'd be happy having a one-night stand with

31

me and then having to sit at a table with your brother and pretend nothing happened while we pull the Christmas crackers and chat with your family?"

Okay, when he puts it like that. My hands fidget in my lap.

"I didn't think so. Because if you feel a fraction for me what I feel for you, it wouldn't be anywhere close to being enough." He doesn't say anything more, instead, he rests his head back against his headrest, shuts his eyes and lets out a deep, exasperated breath.

Feeling defeated and embarrassed, I hop out of the truck so I don't have to face any further rejection. I don't think I could take it.

"Don't worry about it, I'll find someone else. You can forget this conversation ever happened." Tears prick my eyes as I slam the door and walk away from him.

I really am pathetic, aren't I? Thirteen years have passed since I first put myself out there with him and I haven't learned my lesson. Only this time it stings more because whatever the second reason he had for staying away from me, I'm not enough to overcome it.

"Zara, wait!" he calls out, jogging up my garden path to catch me as I reach the small steps leading to my front door. He spins me in his arms like I'm weightless, taking my breath away and not letting me go. When our eyes meet beneath my poor excuse for a security light, the spark I've been searching for tonight surges through me, setting my skin on fire beneath his gaze. His brows tighten when he sees the moisture in my eyes and his voice softens. "I can handle Jackson. I... I can't cope with letting you walk away and missing the chance to show you exactly how you should have been treated this entire time," he tells me, tucking a strand of hair behind my ear. "Get some sleep tonight, I'll call you in the morning when you've got a clear head."

The only sign I'm still breathing is the puffs of breath that appear in the icy air between us.

He takes advantage of my stunned silence and kisses me softly on the cheek before walking backwards towards his truck. I'm rooted in the same spot until he leans against the bonnet, waiting for me to open my front door.

Opening the door is a challenge since I've lost all basic motor skills, and I fumble with the keys until eventually it slides into the lock.

"Goodnight, Zara," he calls out, his smile soft and bright, the smile that was missing earlier.

I offer a wave before I disappear inside, closing the door behind me.

"Oh...my...fuck," I say out loud. I rest my back against the cold wood and slide to the floor, not moving until long after I hear him pull away.

Chapter Five

Noah

I'm not exaggerating when I say Jackson will murder me slowly and painfully for violating his sweet baby sister when he finds out. Because he will find out, there's no doubt about it, because if I get my way, Zara will be mine. Or I'll be hers, more like.

At six a.m., after a night of restless sleep and filthy dreams of me and Zara, I give up trying to sleep and make my way downstairs, flicking on the coffee machine as I go.

I want someone to fuck me thoroughly while telling me to "take their cock like a good girl".

That comment almost put me in an early grave because fuck…hearing those words come out of her mouth was like heaven and I need more of it.

To hell with consequences, I pick up my phone on the off chance she's awake and text her.

Noah: Are you awake?
Zara: Sadly, yes. I'm getting ready for work.

Instead of replying by text and risking her not seeing it, I dial her number and thankfully, she answers on the second ring.

"You should call in sick to work," I say before she can even finish saying hello.

"Good morning to you too." She laughs and I'm glad to see there's no awkwardness between us after her tipsy confessions and my declaration of my feelings for her.

"Were you serious last night? About you and me?"

An anxious knot forms in my stomach as I await her answer.

"Yes," she says. "Were you?"

"Yeah, I was."

"Cool." I feel her cringe down the phone, which makes me grin like a lovesick teenager. "Ugh, I don't think I've ever said cool in all my life."

"Zara McIntosh… Will you call in sick to work and come on an adventure with me, please?" I ask her nicely this time, not wanting to appear forceful. Not that I'd ever make her do anything she didn't want to do, but I know her ex-husband, and I don't want her to think I'm anything like him.

"An adventure does sound way more fun than going to work and pretending to be still married to the boss. But I have responsibilities here, Noah. I can't up and leave the Wednesday before Christmas."

"Fuck the lot of them. I know for a fact you've never taken a sick day – you deserve it. I've watched you for years and I see how you overwork yourself and go above and beyond for that man and his career. Do something for you for once. Besides, it's Christmas, no one gives a fuck about a shitty politician at this time of year anyways."

I'm glad she laughs because I realise too late that she could take offence since she's literally in charge of protecting his image.

"Besides the election happening in January." She pauses "Out of interest, what kind of adventure do you suggest we have? We can't exactly parade around in public, we've never been seen alone together, it'll stand out if Jackson isn't with us."

"I know a place, out in Kielder. A cottage that we can go to where we can hike and stargaze, and you know...hang out."

"Is that what the kids call it these days?"

"I could say I plan to eat you out like it's my last meal, if that's better?"

I assume she's just taken a drink because she splutters and chokes for a second before regaining control.

"I can't believe I'm doing this." She laughs. "You're right, I've never called in sick before and I should do something for myself for once."

"Is that a yes?" My grin is so wide my cheeks are aching.

"What time can you pick me up?" I can hear the excitement in her voice and that alone has my spirits soaring.

"Eleven. I've got to sort some stuff out first. Pack for a few days and bring your hiking boots. Tell them you've got a stomach bug or something super disgusting, so they don't try and guilt you into going into work."

"Okay." She laughs as though she can't believe this is

happening. I can't believe this is happening. "I'll see you soon."

After packing my own bag, I hop in the car and head to the supermarket for supplies. I take care of the practical stuff first and then head to the pharmacy aisle.

I've never paid much attention here, always opting for the same old, bog-standard condoms, but the variety is outstanding now that I'm taking notice.

Ribbed, dotted, multi-textured. I grab a selection.

Lube? We might need it... I'll get some in case.

Vibrating cock ring? Why the hell not?! It's Christmas after all.

A small silver bullet vibrator catches my eye and I grab one of those too because it's always been a fantasy of mine to use one on a woman. After a very awkward teenage boy rings up my items at the till—why I didn't go to the self-checkout I'll never know—I make the short drive to Zara's cottage.

Guilt gnaws at my stomach when I drive past her brother's house and then her parents' place. What would they think if they knew what I had planned for their daughter?

Yeah, I've got a decent-sized bank account after an investment paid off, which is important to her parents, but I don't really fit with the family aesthetic and they certainly wouldn't approve of me as a prospective partner for Zara. I'm not as upper crust as Colin is.

Zara opens the front door before I even step out onto the kerb. She's carrying a small suitcase and a leather backpack, her hiking boots are tied together by the laces and are hanging from her shoulder, and she's wearing a big, beautiful smile on her face.

It's enough to dissolve the tension I felt only moments ago thinking about her family.

"Hey," she says when I reach her.

"Hi." I can't help but grin back at her as I take her bags and carry them to the truck, excitement filling the atmosphere around us. Like a gentleman, I open her door and help her climb in before jogging to my side and joining her, shutting the cool air out.

"Did you pre-warm the seat for me?" she asks, snuggling into her seat.

"Yeah, it's a chilly morning, I didn't want you to be too cold." I lean forward, opening the glove compartment. "I didn't know which road trip sweets you'd like so I got a few different kinds."

"A few? There are more sweets in here than a Wilkinson's Pick 'n' Mix stand."

She rummages around, settling on the bag of mini flumps, then smiling as she pops a marshmallow into her mouth.

I pull away, leaving her street and the perfectly arranged Christmas lights belonging to her neighbours in the rear-view mirror. I think Zara's cottage was the only one with no sign of any festive decorations.

"So, how did work take it?" I ask as we cross the town line on our way to Kielder.

"Not well. Colin has a big Christmas Day speech, and I left the work with the intern," She shrugs and looks thoughtfully out of the window. "I need a new job, don't I?"

"Are you happy still working there?" She shakes her head. "Then I'd say you need a new job."

She turns in her seat to face me. "I don't want to talk about Colin when we get to the cabin, so I'm going to get it all out now. You can ask as many questions as you want because I don't want to think about him from the second we get out of this truck."

"You don't have to tell me if you don't want to." I reach over and thread my fingers through hers, doing my best to show her support and keep my attention on the road.

"I want to. Because you need to understand this isn't some rebound thing to get back at him. This is a me thing and it has nothing to do with Colin. We split up six months ago when I caught him cheating. He moved out with zero arguments and has been living with his mistress ever since. Our families have no idea and he wants to keep it that way until after the local election in January so it doesn't tarnish his reputation."

"Seriously? Zara, why have you been going through this alone? Jackson would have supported you."

"We both know Jackson has been a little pre-occupied lately." So, I'm not the only one Jackson has been distant with; I'm still waiting for a call back from last night.

"I'm your friend as much as I am Jackson's, you could have come to me."

"I always figured you thought of me as Jackson's annoying little sister."

"I did," I tease, and she lets go of my hand dramatically, but I link my fingers with her once again without protest. "Somewhere along the line I started to really like that about you, among other things."

She settles back into her seat with a shy smile, holding my hand tighter and pulling it into her lap as she gets comfortable.

Chapter Six

Zara

A little over an hour after Noah picks me up, he's pulling off the winding country roads through a small opening in the hedgerows onto a crisp gravel driveway.

A collection of chestnut and oak trees lean over the narrow road forming a canopy of empty branches above it. I imagine during the spring and summer months this place would be bursting with vibrant shades of greens. Right now, the snow-covered branches and the flurries of snowflakes in the air look like an image you'd find on a Christmas card.

We drive for a few more minutes before the road opens to a small clearing where a quaint stone cottage stands in the middle of nowhere, complete with a chimney pot and a wooden wrap-around deck.

Have we stepped into a Hallmark Christmas movie? The place is perfect, so beautiful and peaceful. Other than Noah and I climbing out of the truck, the only sounds to be heard are the natural sounds of the forest. Trees creaking and branches rustling, birds chirping happily somewhere in the distance, and a tiny robin that perches on the hanging bird feeder, unbothered by our arrival.

Even the air out here tastes and smells so much cleaner!

"It's amazing, isn't it?" Noah wraps his strong arms around me from behind, and it feels so natural. I stroke his forearms, leaning into his embrace as my back presses against his front. When his face nuzzles my neck, my heart is fit to burst with the show of affection.

"It's so beautiful and quiet I swear even my thoughts are clearer. It's exactly what I need."

"I'll bring you here as often as you like."

"Do you own this place?" I ask, glancing back at him over my shoulder.

"Yeah, I bought it a few years back. Shall I give you the tour?"

He takes my hand in his and leads me up the few wooden steps to the deck.

"Wow." I gasp when he opens the front door; inside the small cottage is decorated how I imagine Santa's grotto to be! The more I look and walk around the cosy living room, the more I see.

An eight-foot tree decorated in red and gold is twinkling in the corner, and coordinating garlands are draped over the mantelpiece and sash windows. There are candles and poinsettias everywhere, and is that a hot chocolate station?

"Christmas is important to you, so I had someone come to decorate this morning before we arrived."

"You did this all for me?"

"Yeah, it's too much, isn't it? Shit, sorry, I've never

brought anyone here before, and I know you love Christmas, so I wanted to make it cosy and special."

"Noah, this is perfect," I reassure him. "I didn't decorate at home this year. Colin used to get the decorations out of the loft and I couldn't manage by myself so I didn't bother."

I can't believe he did all this in such a short period of time and just because he thought I'd like it.

"I want to show you the best part, my favourite part."

I follow as he walks to a set of double French windows that look out onto the back decking.

Beyond the twinkling lights wrapped around the wooden terrace and hot tub outside, is the most beautiful view I've ever seen. Where the front of the cottage is secluded and sheltered by trees, the back looks out onto acres of snow-covered rolling fields.

"In the summer, these fields grow wheat and rapeseed and a few in the distance grow heather. But now, seeing them covered in snow, it feels like we could be anywhere else in the world."

As if the movement is choreographed, we step closer to each other. I weave my arms around his neck and relax into him as he pulls me closer. I'm shorter than him, so I tilt my neck so I can look into the depths of his brown eyes.

"I'm so glad I called you last night."

"I'm so glad you called me."

He lowers his face closer to mine, leaving a hair's width between us as though he's savouring the moment before his lips brush mine. When he kisses me, it's as though I'm the person he's been waiting for his entire life. In reality, I think it might be the other way around.

There's more heat, more spark, more everything in this kiss than I've ever experienced and all he's done is kiss me.

He draws himself away from my lips, taking a moment to assess my reaction. It's nowhere near enough for either of us, so this time we come together in a crash of bodies. I deepen the kiss, parting my lips in invitation. He lifts me from my feet, carrying me to the rustic kitchen table and settling me on the edge as he stands between my thighs. His tongue caresses mine in delicious strokes, and I moan into his mouth.

"Zara," he whispers my name with so much emotion my heart is fit to burst.

"Don't stop," I plead.

He lets out a low groan, kissing along my jawline and down my neck, giving in to his desires once again. I moan as his hands explore the curves and dips of my body, willing his hands to journey lower where I need him most right now. But instead, he stops entirely.

"I should get the firewood," he says, resting his forehead against mine. "It's freezing in here."

"Keep kissing me, that'll keep us warm."

He chuckles when my teeth chatter, betraying me.

"I need to start a fire so when you're spread out in front of me, ready to devour, you're nice and warm and relaxed." His voice is low and seductive, and I whimper once more.

"Okay, that sounds like a good plan."

He pulls me in for a final, soft kiss and helps me down from the table.

I'm floating on air as I empty my case. I place the lingerie I packed neatly in the empty drawer in his bedroom, and the rest of my clothes I hang next to his in the wardrobe.

Unlike the rest of the cottage, there are no Christmas decorations in the bedroom. There are a few stunning photographs of some familiar North East landmarks, a stack of well-loved photography books on the bedside table and a string of fairy lights woven around the wrought-iron bed frame.

When I'm finished unpacking and having a snoop, I make my way back out to the living room. The fluffy tartan blanket from the back of the sofa is warm and inviting as I sit on one of the chairs with a view out the French windows where Noah is putting on quite the show.

I finally understand the term "lumber snack".

If that kiss hadn't turned me on beyond the point of no return…this would have done it.

Noah yielding an axe has to be one of the sexiest things I've ever seen.

His jacket and jumper have both been discarded to the side, despite the near constant snowfall, as he swings the axe down, effortlessly chopping a thick log in half. I can see the sweat running down the taught muscles of his tanned neck. His forearms straining from the effort.

A fire spreads through me and settles in a low hum between

my legs, gaining in intensity every time he swings the axe. His lips quirk up into a smile when he spots me practically fanning myself from behind the glass. There's no need for the blanket anymore because when he winks at me, actually fucking winks like he's the hero in a romance novel, I almost burst into flames.

"See something you like out there?" he asks, grinning at me when he comes in with a pile of wood cradled in his arms.

"Yeah, you could say that." I laugh.

He tosses the wood on the floor next to the fireplace before leaning down and kissing me.

"I'm going to get this fire going and then I need a shower. Is that okay?"

"I mean, if you wanted to stay like this, I would not mind one bit."

He chuckles. "I'm a sweaty mess."

"Yeah, and I think I've unlocked a secret kink I didn't know I had."

"Good job we're here alone then, there's plenty of time to explore that later, babe."

Babe.

He called me "babe".

One tiny four-letter word and my heart is pounding in overdrive again.

Chapter Seven

Noah

"This is not fair!" Zara whines as I beat her at my favourite board game: Frustration. The sun set quickly a few hours ago and since then, we've played Cluedo, which she won at an impressive speed, and Monopoly, which we quickly decided isn't the best game to play on our first date. "Ugh, god, you are so frustrating." She pouts.

"Why do you think the game is called Frustration, Zara?"

She bangs her tiny fist against the dome, clicking the little dice over and over again until she gets the number she wants.

"You're so cute when you're being bratty."

Although her frown is deep, the laughter in her eyes is hard to hide. Where her brother wears his heart on his sleeve, she shows it in her soul.

"Okay, why don't we try something different?" I pull her from her seat and onto my lap, my dick springing to life as she purposely grinds against me getting comfortable.

"How long can we stay here?" she asks, watching the falling snow outside. Her arms are draped around my neck as I run my hands up and down her back, loving the way her skin puckers up into goosebumps.

"We can stay here as long as you want. I don't have to get back for anything, so how long we stay is your call."

She turns back to me with another megawatt smile and gently scrapes her fingernails through the hair at the nape of my neck, the sensation sending ripples of pleasure deep into my core.

"I'm beginning to think this is all a perfect dream."

"It's real, babe." I brush my lips against hers.

With both hands on her bum, I yank her towards me, making her gasp as our centres meet, showing her the true effect she has on me. Her eyes widen eagerly as she feels my erection press against her. She presses her palm to my face, stroking me softly as she watches my reaction to her rolling her hips against me, teasing both of us.

"Oh, believe me, I could tell last night when you almost burst out of your jeans. In these grey sweatpants, you're mouth-watering."

"You have no idea how much restraint I showed last night, Zara. You've been the star of every fantasy I've had since you walked into your brother's birthday party six months ago. Something had changed about you, you seemed to walk on air and, man, that fucking smile, it nearly killed me off. I hated knowing that I've been developing feelings for another man's wife. But all this time...you could have been mine."

"The day of Jackson's party was the day Colin moved out," she tells me. "I told you, he did me a favour. I felt like I was a new woman that night."

"As much as I'd love to beat the living daylights out of him for doing this to you, his loss is my gain." I comb her hair through my fingers, letting it flow like liquid gold over her shoulder.

"This is crazy, right? How quickly this has happened."

"It feels right, though. At least for me, it does."

"Me too," she whispers against my lips. The soft skin of her nose brushes against mine. Our kiss starts slow and soft but when she opens her mouth to let my tongue slide against hers, we break. She moans into my mouth when I move her hips harder, pressing my dick against her.

"I hope you brought condoms because I was so flustered this morning it didn't even cross my mind."

"Don't worry, I did. But we don't need one yet, because as long as you're still ok with this…I've got other things in mind for you tonight."

She nods as I stand and carry her to the faux fur rug in front of the fire, laying her on her back as I nudge her thighs apart. The red and orange flames cast a warm glow across her. I lean back on my heels and strip away my shirt, throwing it on the back of the sofa.

"Oh, my god." Her eyes burn me as they drink me in, taking in each line of muscle. I'd be lying if I said it didn't feed my ego seeing her reaction to me. Her fingertips trace every line. "Are you real?"

"I built a home gym," I tell her. "I work out a lot."

"Whatever you're doing in there, it's working."

She tosses her satin pyjama shirt away, leaving her in a white lace bustier and pyjama shorts that leave nothing to the imagination.

"You're so beautiful, Zara," I whisper against her lips as I lower her back to the floor, her back hitting the soft rug.

"No one's ever called me beautiful like that before."

"Like what?"

"Like you actually meant it," she tells me. Her vulnerability hits me.

"I do mean it and you'd better get used to it because I'll make sure you never forget it."

We get lost in our kiss, the fire crackling in the background as we make out on the floor in front of it.

I've never been with a woman like this; I've never taken my time and let myself enjoy being in the moment, but with Zara, I never want this moment to end.

Chapter Eight

Zara

How long we spend on the floor kissing like teenagers is anyone's guess. I'm so lost in Noah that time means nothing to me anymore.

It's crazy, but I feel more alive now than I ever have.

All my life, I've made decisions with my head. Marrying Colin was a smart decision I made for my parents. It was a safe decision because our marriage meant a major contract was signed for my family's business to provide construction work for the local government.

With Noah, this is all heart and body.

I throw my sensible head out the window, telling myself I don't care that this could end terribly if it got out that I'm here, with a man who's not my "husband".

Because I've never wanted anything more in my life than I want Noah, and he knows it. I moan as he traces circles around my nipples through the thin fabric of my lingerie, my arousal increasing as his thumb brushes over the sensitive peak.

"This is all for you, Zara, tell me what you want." He kisses down my neck and along my collarbone, his short beard grazing my skin, and his lips pushing down my bra strap before repeating the motion on the other side and lowering the cups, releasing my breasts.

"I-I don't know. I don't know what I've been living without. There's so much I want to feel."

He leans back on his heels and undoes the tie of my white satin pyjama shorts.

"Can I?" He waits until I nod before lifting my hips so he can pull them over my bum and down my legs. He tosses them and they land with the rest of our clothes strewn over the back of the couch.

His grey sweatpants reveal his reaction to seeing me and, fuck, he looks…big, especially when he dips his hand beneath the fabric to readjust himself.

"Then tell me, do you want my fingers or my mouth first?"

Oh god, even his words make the ache between my legs throb faster.

"I want both, but I want your fingers first." I barely manage to breathe out the words as his beautiful brown eyes feast on my matching thong that he slowly peels away.

"I like that idea." He brings his large hands between us, pushing my legs wider apart. "I can't wait to taste you."

"I like that," I say as he slowly rubs his hands up my thighs, coming closer and closer to where I desperately want him. "Keep talking to me."

He grins a wicked smile. "You like it when I talk to you?"

He leans over me, kissing me softly as he brushes his fingers across my clit.

"Fuck!" he moans, nibbling on my ear. "You're so wet, babe."

There's that word again, the one that has me free-falling every time he says it.

When he slides his middle finger down over my clit and to my entrance, I cry out from the sensation. It's beautiful torture; I need more and he knows it.

He pulls his finger into his mouth and moans. "You taste so fucking good, Zara."

"Oh fuck!" I moan as he returns two fingers to me, brushing my wetness all over, making me feel things I've never felt all while maintaining eye contact with me like he's watching carefully for any and all reaction.

"Has anyone ever touched you here?" he asks, sliding his fingers lower, giving me more pressure as he rubs all of me.

"Never, oh fuck! Please don't stop," I beg as the new sensations hit me as he rubs his fingers against me. I never saw the appeal of ass play before now but as his thumb rolls around my clit, giving me double the sensation, I never want to go without it again.

"That's it," he encourages my cries. He takes my hand and guides it to my breast, showing me how to toy with my own nipples. "Tell me what you want from me now."

"I want your mouth; I want you to go down on me."

He grins as he plants open-mouthed kisses all down my

body until he settles between my legs.

"Look at me." I prop up onto my elbows to watch as he lowers his face to my glistening heat. He inhales, moaning happily before he makes contact.

The first swirl of his tongue is enough to have me seeing stars. The way he carefully keeps me teetering on the edge as he devours me has to be witchcraft. He pushes a finger into me followed by another as our moans fill the air. He sounds like he's enjoying this as much as I am and it thrills me. I feel unstoppable; I didn't know it could be this good. Even though I'm the one being pleasured, he's enjoying it too which makes me feel incredible and sexy.

"Oh god! Noah! Yes!" I cry out as my orgasm builds to the point of explosion. His hair is in my white-knuckled fists and my back arches from the floor as he continues his rhythmic motions across all of me. He licks and rubs me all while pounding his fingers deep inside of me, hitting that all-important spot.

And then it happens. I can't take any more. It's like I'm falling and flying at the same time. His name explodes from me in loud cries as my climax rips through my body. My vision blurs and my heart rate soars as my orgasm reaches its pinnacle.

I must black out or something because the next thing I'm fully aware of is Noah's face next to mine whispering praise in my ear as he nuzzles his nose against me.

His fingers encourage the remainder of my orgasm from me as I continue to spasm against them. I'm a melted puddle; I can barely move, so I don't, I enjoy the sensations he's giving me.

"Oh fuck," I whisper. He kisses me lazily as my body slowly comes back to life.

"Yeah, you can say that again." His eyes drop to his crotch, evidence of his own release there.

"Did you...?"

"Yeah, that's never happened before but watching you come apart like that, I couldn't hold back either, babe."

And just like that, I feel like I could take on the fucking world.

Chapter Nine

Noah

After we take a long shower together, I make sure Zara is wrapped up warm before I bring her outside into the fresh winter air. The snow has moved on and the dark sky is clear, making way for the entire solar system to make an appearance above us.

"This is so beautiful," she says as she lies in front of me, both of us wrapped in a warm blanket on the outdoor lounger looking up at the twinkling stars. "I've never seen the stars so bright."

I kiss her temple softly as she lets out a content sigh.

"Do you come here often?" she asks, and I laugh at what sounds like a cheesy chat-up line. "Okay, I heard that." She laughs.

"I come every few weeks. When Dad is in a bad way at the care home, I tend to take a day or two to myself. It doesn't help him when I'm there if he's too confused or doesn't remember me and I hate sitting at home knowing there's nothing I can do about it."

"Noah, I'm so sorry." She turns to sit on her knees and face me. "Is that why you wanted to come here, to get away too?"

"Yesterday was a really tough day."

"Why didn't you say something? I'm so sorry I made you

drive all that way to pick me up and deal with my drama last night when it was the last thing you needed."

"I didn't say anything because, if you can't tell, I'm not great at sharing my thoughts and feelings and shit. I normally talk to Jackson about this stuff but like you said, he's a bit distracted lately and never called me back. And please don't ever apologise for last night. If it weren't for last night I wouldn't have you here now, finally in my arms."

"Do you want to talk about yesterday? You don't have to, but if it's something you feel like you can share with me, I'd like to be the person you turn to when you need someone to listen."

"I don't know what I did to deserve you." I kiss her softly, sitting up on the lounger so we're at eye level. "Dad asked me if I had a girlfriend. When I said no, he said he didn't want me to be alone all and that the happiest memories of his life were with my mam. When he started thinking about her it triggered a reaction, and he forgot me. Mentally, he was back in a time when I didn't exist. It killed me to see him shouting for her so desperately. I knew I was only making things worse so I left."

I look down at our entwined hands, unable to look her in the eye.

"Oh, Noah. It's not your fault," she whispers, tears glistening in her eyes as though she can hear my thoughts. "And I'm sure he didn't mean it how it sounded. Your dad loves you so much. I remember when I came to watch you and Jackson graduate from uni. I watched you with your dad and he was so incredibly proud of you. If I were with my parents and we'd run into him in the street or at a neighbourhood party, his eyes would light up every time your name was mentioned. You were everything to him and you still are deep down. It's awful what's happening to him. You're both wonderful, kind and loving men and you don't deserve this pain."

"I didn't realise how badly I needed to hear that," I say, swallowing back my emotion. "The home he's in is the best money can buy and the nurses are amazing with him."

"You're a wonderful son, Noah. Don't ever forget that."

"Thank you."

"What do you do when you come out here alone?" she asks.

"I take photographs. After I sold the patent for my computer when I was twenty-three. I invested the money in a digital online communications start-up. This was pre-covid obviously, and for a few years it did well, bringing in cash that I was able to save up and then, as you know, it paid out big time over the pandemic. I left my job and I'm able to live off pretty much the interest alone. I bought this place and started to teach myself how to take photographs and how to edit them. It's something I'd always wanted to do yet never had the time."

"The pictures hanging inside, did you take those?" She snuggles back into my side as we face each other on the sun lounger.

"Yeah, they're all mine. I didn't think you'd noticed them."

"Of course, I did, they're amazing. The picture of the night sky with the Milky Way in the bedroom, that's my favourite. It reminds me of this moment right now." Her enthusiasm is contagious. "You're so talented, Noah!"

"I'm glad you think so." I laugh, trying to play off the flush in my cheeks. "I've never told anyone that before. Not even Jackson knows about this cabin or my photography."

"Why?"

"Because I liked having something to myself, that only I knew about."

"You brought me here."

"You're the first person I've wanted to let into this part of my life."

She kisses me softly on the lips. It's a short and sweet kiss, but in it is so much more unspoken emotion. I've shared everything with her tonight, my feelings and worries about my dad, my passion for photography. She didn't run away scared. She stayed.

"Come on, it's getting late. Let me take you to bed."

Chapter Ten

Zara

When I wake the next morning, the sun is barely peeking above the horizon in the distance.

I reach out for Noah but, although still warm, the bed is empty. The hoody he wore yesterday hangs over the chair in the corner of the room. When I pull it on, his deliciously woody scent washes over me. I never want to take this thing off, it's cosy and reminds me of him.

When I wander out of the bedroom, I find him crouched down by the fireplace in the living room stoking the growing flames.

Although real-life Noah is sexy and funny and kind, Christmas cottage Noah is otherworldly.

I stand and lean against the door frame, watching as he tends to the flames, the muscles in his back rippling and tensing beneath his tanned skin the same way they did last night when he crawled over me in bed and made my dreams come true…twice.

Sensing my appreciative gaze, he turns to face me. My filthy thoughts must be written all over my face, because he grins and stalks towards me like a predator coming for his very willing, extremely horny prey.

"Good morning, beautiful," he says, his voice still husky from sleep. He leans in to kiss me, but I stop him with a hand over his mouth. He grunts as I slap him in the face with my palm.

"Sorry! But I haven't brushed my teeth!"

"I don't care." He grabs my wrists and, in one swift movement, pins them above my head so my spine is pressed against the door frame.

"Oh my god!" I moan as he kisses my neck and nibbles on my ear lobe, his hands stroking down my arms, over my breasts and down my waist where he holds me against him. When he captures my mouth with his, my body turns to jelly.

"Why are you out of bed?" he asks as he hooks his hands on the back of my thighs and carries me back into his bedroom, his fingers brushing against my skin, teasing me as he gets closer to my centre. When he reaches me, he finds me wet and naked beneath his hoody.

He lowers me down against my pillow before climbing over me and caging me with his arms.

"I want to show you something first," he says as I try and wriggle closer to him, desperate for some friction. Three orgasms less than twelve hours ago and I need more, like an addict.

He jumps out of bed and pulls a camera out of a bag in the wardrobe before settling in next to me and pulling the covers back over us.

"I took some photos the other day and haven't edited them

yet. I thought you might like to see and then maybe we can go for a walk in the snow and take some pictures together?"

"I'd love that." I snuggle into his side as he wraps his big arms around me.

It's not only the orgasms, I'm quickly becoming addicted to this feeling of being safe, wanted, and sexy.

Colin never wanted to snuggle in the morning; he woke up at five a.m. every single day. Even on weekends he never slept in past seven and I always felt judged for needing more sleep. God forbid if I wanted an afternoon nap.

With Noah, there's no rush to start the day at all. All he wants is to be with me, in the moment.

I should stop comparing Noah to Colin because there is no comparison at all. He presses a few buttons on the camera and the first photograph pops up on the screen.

"Wow, it's stunning," I say, looking at the shot of the Northern Lights dancing across the North East coastline.

"I drove to Bamburgh and Seahouses the other day and took these. It was incredible, and if it's clear enough tonight, they'll be back again. It's a dark sky spot here so I like our chances."

He flicks through a few more pictures and each one is more impressive than the last, perfect even without any editing.

"You should display these photographs, Noah. You're so talented, people would love to see them."

"I don't know about that." There's a shyness in his voice I've never heard before and that in itself tells me how passionate he is about his photography.

I hook my legs over him and lift myself up so I'm straddling him. His hand automatically finds the curve of my waist beneath his hoody and as I adjust my position across him, I finally find that friction I crave.

He raises an eyebrow, smirking as he watches me.

"Would you ever photograph people?" I ask, biting my lip.

"I'd photograph you. Especially right now, with the sunrise, you look like a fucking mirage sent to drive me crazy."

He snaps a few pictures of me smiling as I sit on top of him. For the first time, I feel confident. I don't care that my hair is a mess or that I'm not wearing make-up. I still feel beautiful.

He shows me the picture, and...I look good. The golden sun streams through the open blinds and reflects off my hair, the peak of my nipple stretching the fabric of his hoody. It looks like a picture of a model glowing with happiness. Something I'm not at all used to.

Happiness.

His hand travels up my waist so he can draw his thumb around my nipple, sending a zap of pleasure between my legs.

"Keep taking photos as you do that." I gasp as he grinds his erection into me from below.

I peel off the hoody with two hands and throw it onto the ground, revealing my complete nakedness.

"Fuck, Zara. Is this ok?" he asks, camera still in hand as he watches me play with my own nipples.

"Don't stop taking pictures."

"Can I touch you?" he asks, groaning as I move against him.

I bite my lower lip as I lift my hips to allow his hand to reach between us, then his middle finger circles and nudges my clit before sliding inside of me.

"Oh, fuck," I moan. "Where are the condoms?"

He reaches into the drawer, pulling out a box still wrapped in cellophane, ripping it with his teeth until the condoms spill everywhere.

I grab one and tear it open with my teeth, only stopping to cry out as he slides a second finger inside of me.

Leaning back, I take his straining dick in my hand and roll on the condom, loving the way he throbs in my hand. I knew from last night that he's big, but since last night was, in his words, "reserved for my pleasure", this is the first time I'm seeing him.

"Oh fuck," he says as I stroke him with my firm fist, a bead of moisture forming on his tip.

"Keep taking those photos," I remind him with a wicked smile as I line myself up ready to slide onto him.

Slowly, I lower myself, taking him inch by inch. I'm met with a delicious filling sensation as my body stretches to accommodate him until finally, he's fully sheathed by me.

This connection is a feeling I've never experienced and not just physically, but between our souls. Noah and I are compatible in every way.

"I don't want this to be the last time we do something like this, Noah," I tell him honestly, crying out as he grinds up, rubbing my clit against his base. "I want this forever." It's like the chemistry between us brings out my honesty like a truth serum as I ride him faster and faster until the camera is long forgotten. I shouldn't say stuff like that during sex, but the words tumble out of me.

He moans and meets each of my thrusts, guiding me with his large hands on my bum, his fingers biting into my skin.

"You mean that, Zara?"

He flips us around so he's towering over me, caging me in with his arms on either side of my head. I'm impressed he's able to do it without breaking our connection.

He thrusts in hard as I cry out in pleasure from the new angle, reaching a place deep inside me I didn't even know existed.

"Because if you mean that, babe, I promise I'll give you everything. Who gives a fuck about the consequences. I can talk to Jackson, I can tell him how I feel about you, and he'll have to deal with that because if you'll have me, I'm yours."

I crush my lips against his as he gives me everything I ever wanted. Love, passion and security.

"Give it all to me, Noah, I can take it," I tell him with a naughty grin, thinking back to that first conversation we had in his truck. His expression changes, his eyes shining filthily as he lowers his face to mine.

"That's it. Fuck, Zara, you're such a good girl," he growls, his voice thick and gravelly as he thrusts into me hard and fast.

"Oh fuck!" I moan in response because this thing between us just got impossibly hotter. We give each other everything we have until we both crash over the edge together, our joint orgasms bringing us closer and detonating stars behind my eyes.

This is it; this is what I've been searching for, and I found it in the unlikeliest of places. My brother's best friend.

Ellie White

Chapter Eleven

Noah

Zara takes my hand as we walk through the secluded forest around the cabin looking for the perfect spot to take some snowy pictures. I gave her one of my old cameras to use so she can take some pictures of her own.

She looks adorable in her woolly hat and oversized scarf, smiling at me from behind her lens.

"Smile, Noah," she sings as she snaps a photo of me taking a photo, so I take one of her too.

We walk along the tree line and despite it being freezing cold, the sun is shining low in the sky, projecting light and shadows across the rolling hills in the distance.

"How's this?" she asks, showing me a landscape picture she's taken.

"Wow, Zara. That's amazing." Although the screen is small on this camera, I can see the clear level of detail she's managed to capture. "You're a natural."

"Thank you," she says, her chest puffing out proudly as she grins down at her work, and I snap another picture of her. She's quickly becoming my favourite subject to photograph. It's hard not to see the carefree smile creeping in more and more the longer we spend out here, freed from the stress she's under at home. She looks at ease among the evergreens, her cheeks and nose pink from the cold, and her eyes wide and sparkling with wonderment, like she belongs here.

I snap another few photographs of her as she inspects some of the winter wildflowers that have popped up from beneath the snow blanket before lifting her camera again.

"Are you actually going to take photos of something that isn't me?" She grins, not even looking up from her camera.

"I'm taking photos of the most beautiful thing around here."

"Smooth." She laughs as stands up straight and wraps her arms around my neck. "You already have me, Noah. You don't need to flatter me."

"It's true. You are the most beautiful thing here. And you need to get better at receiving compliments."

"I'm not used to it." She looks away, her cheeks pink.

"I know, which is why I'm going to keep giving them to you. Because you need to hear how gorgeous—" I punctuate with a kiss. "Sexy—" Another kiss. "And completely, soul shatteringly perfect you are for me."

I capture her lips with mine as I tangle her hair around my fingers. When she moans into my mouth, I suddenly regret that we got out of bed today at all.

"You're perfect for me too," she says when we pull away

to catch our breath, holding each other closely.

A vibrating in my pocket grabs my attention, and I pull out my phone, a cold fear sinking in that it's Dad's care home, even though I've been in constant contact with them since we got here through messages.

"It's Jackson," I say, and Zara's face pales. "Should I answer it?"

"What does he want?"

"I don't know. I guess he's finally calling me back."

"You should answer it," she tells me.

"Alright, mate," I answer before it clicks over to my voicemail, putting it on speaker so Zara can hear.

"Hi, mate. How's things? I had a missed call," Jackson says. "Sorry, I've been so preoccupied with Christmas and Nikole and work, and I've just gotten a chance to call you back."

"Ah, it's no bother. It was—"

"Babe, can you please concentrate? We need to discuss the seating." Nikole's shrill voice rings out in the background.

"I'm on the phone with Noah," Jackson calls back to her. "Sorry, mate. What were you saying?"

"It's just... Dad had a bad—"

"Jackson, are you going to take this seriously or not?" Nikole screeches. "You always do this! This is important to me and you don't even care. How can I do this if you don't support me." I glance over at Zara who is scowling at the phone, doing her best to bite her tongue. Her losing her temper and outing us like this is the last thing we need.

"Sorry, mate, I'm going to have to go. We can talk on Christmas Day. You're still coming to Mam and Dad's for dinner, right?" Zara gives me an eager nod before miming that we'll go together and that has me smiling again.

"Yeah, mate. I'll see you at Christmas. I have something important I want to tell you and I need to do it in person, so it'd be good to get a beer beforehand?"

"Okay, mate, sounds good."

"Jackson!"

"See you then." He sighs before hanging up the phone.

The phone cuts off, leaving Zara and me in total silence as we both process the phone call. It's a standard call I've had with Jackson lately, and Zara's expression reassures me that his change in attitude isn't all in my head.

"He's acting like a fucking dickhead," she finally bites.

"He's preoccupied. You heard him. Work, Nikole, life." I'm not sure why I'm defending him, he's been a shitty friend lately.

"No, he's not, he's prioritising his fucking crazy girlfriend over his best friend. Like, I get it, he's in a new relationship, but when was the last time you spoke to him? Like properly spoke to him, or hung out?"

"A few weeks ago...maybe a month or so," I tell her, getting the feeling this isn't only about my experience anymore. "When was the last time you spoke to him?"

"Other than him calling me at the office to ask about the election coming up and for other work-related calls...a few months ago, maybe more. I don't remember the last time he came to the house."

Jackson is a political journalist, so it makes sense for him to call Zara for work, she's head of PR for Colin; she arranges all his press contact and appearances. But the fact he hasn't been around her outside of that is telling. He knows her better than anyone and would have noticed a difference in her the past six months for sure. If he'd been to her house, he'd have seen that Colin had moved out and that his sister needed some support.

It's hard not to resent him for his behaviour.

"I'll talk to him, see if I can find out what's going on with him. Because we both know this isn't him."

"Yeah. You're right," she says with a sigh, taking my hand and continuing our walk. "I was thinking...do you think we could stay here until Christmas Eve?"

"Anything you want. I don't think I'm ready to go back to the real world yet either."

Chapter Twelve

Zara

"One large hot chocolate with a mountain of whipped cream and mini marshmallows," Noah says, joining me in front of the fire and placing our tray of drinks next to me.

We've been here five days now, enjoying each other's company, going out for hikes and exploring the woods around the cabin. We've talked, kissed, and had mind-blowing sex until we both pass out completely exhausted. Then we wake up and do it all again the next day.

It's the perfect escape.

For four nights the Northern Lights have been forecast but we've not seen a single flicker and looking outside at the clouds tonight I'm beginning to lose hope.

"Don't pout, babe." Noah laughs when he notices. "The clouds might clear. And if they don't, I'll take you to see them another time."

He kisses me on the lips, massaging my pout away. He pulls away and leans with his back against the couch like I am, pointing his feet towards the fire in an attempt to defrost our toes. We decided to go out in the darkness to try and get some shots of the stars, but we couldn't see any of those either.

"Come on, Zara, don't do this." He nudges my shoulder playfully with his.

"Do what?" I ask, confused.

"I know you're stressing about going home. But it's Christmas Eve tomorrow. You love Christmas Eve."

"Noah, I don't think I can go back to my life there. Not how it was."

"Then tell me how I can help because you're not going back there alone. We're going back together."

"I'm going to quit my job. On our way home, after we visit your dad, I want you to take me to the office. Colin will be there late, he always is, but I know the office manager will send everyone else home early," I tell him my plan. "I'm going to tell him about us too, and that we need to come clean about our divorce because I'm not going to keep us a secret to protect him."

"You are?"

"Is that okay with you? I figure if I'm going to tell my parents and Jackson about the divorce, then I should give him a heads-up."

"Of course, it is, I don't want to keep us a secret either. I want to shout it from every rooftop in the village!"

I laugh as he pulls me into his arms.

"Let's make the most of our last night here," I tell him. "Let's go to bed."

Chapter Thirteen

Noah

Zara does not need to ask me twice.

I rise to my feet, pulling her with me, kissing her and shedding our clothes as we stumble to our bedroom. I've been saving the toys for tonight since it's our last night here and it's Christmas Eve's eve, so why not celebrate!

"I have a surprise for you," I say as her back hits the mattress, her breasts bouncing, threatening to spill over her bra. She props herself up on her elbows, her bare toes barely grazing the ground as she lies in her underwear.

"A surprise?"

She watches with a keen eye as I jog around the bed and pull out the collection of toys and a condom from the drawer.

"Oooh…" Her eyes widen in excitement as she takes in the picture of the silver bullet vibrator on the box.

"I saw it in the shop and thought it might be good to experiment. I've never used anything like this before."

"Well, I have that exact vibrator in pink so I can tell you exactly what to do with it." She flutters her fingertips across her collarbone, pushing away her bra straps and unclasping her bra at the front, letting it hang open, displaying her perfect pink nipples. I groan as I watch her play with them, my dick springing to life when she moans. "Or I could show you?"

"Fuck, yes."

Wasting no further time, I rip open the box and pull the vibrator out, reading the instructions carefully before I turn it on.

"What's that?" she asks, looking at the second box I'd thrown face down onto the bed. She picks it up and examines it. She draws her already swollen lip into her mouth, biting on it as her eyes meet mine. "Can I put it on you?"

I nod. She takes my excruciatingly hard dick in her hand, stroking me slowly from base to tip. She picks up the condom packet from the bed and rolls that on before stretching the vibrating cock ring around my base with the vibrating bud between my dick and my balls.

"I think that's meant to go on top, for you," I say, watching her hand as she continues to stroke me.

"I have this." She lifts up the vibrator. "You should get to feel something too."

She flicks the switch on the side and the sensations hit me immediately.

"Oh my god, fuck!" I collapse to my knees between her thighs, and she smiles, loving how weak she's made me.

"Shit, I don't think I'm going to last long with this, babe." I readjust the position, releasing some of the pressure but keeping enough to still feel it.

"Don't worry, I won't take long either. Oh, yes!" She sighs in relief when she rubs the tip of the vibrating bullet across her lace-covered clit.

I pull her underwear down her legs, throw them aside and spread her wide, resting one foot on my shoulder, kissing the smooth arch, and the other on the edge of the bed. She's so wet, she's glistening, and it takes all my strength not to devour her right away. The skin of her thighs is so soft as I push closer to her entrance.

Leaning back on one arm, she circles her clit with the vibrator, moaning softly as she picks up the pace of her rhythm.

"That's it. Fuck that looks so good," I encourage her.

"It feels so good," she moans. "I want your fingers inside of me though," she begs as she presses the vibrator harder. "And then when I'm close, I want to come on your cock."

I groan loudly as I grab my dick in my hand, releasing some of the tension built up from the vibrations, using my other hand to push two fingers inside of her, curling them as I stroke her. She cries out at the sensation, her walls clamping tightly around my fingers as I thrust them into her, harder and harder as requested. She's so wet, I glide into her easily, loving the way her arousal drips down my hand. When I let my little finger brush over her tight hole as I continue my thrusts inside of her, she begs me for more. Screaming my name louder than ever before, she praises me and fuck it feels good.

I push the cock ring to its original position, welcoming back the intense vibrations as I glide my fist up and down, up and down.

"That's it, baby, I can feel you getting close. Tell me when I can bury my cock deep inside of you."

"Fuck me, Noah. Now!"

I jump to my feet, hiking her knees up around my waist, and plunge into her in one smooth motion; the vibrator pressed against her clit buzzes against my dick as I enter her.

One deep, hard thrust is all it takes.

As my orgasm wracks through my body, I feel her clench and spasm around me as we cry out together. It's the most intense orgasm I've ever had. White-hot blinding pleasure pulses through my body and with each grinding thrust, I give her everything I've got until we're completely drained and my knees can't support my body anymore.

Zara's limp wrist drops the vibrator to her side as she lazily reaches for me, stroking my face as I collapse on top of her.

I kiss her slowly, connecting with her on a completely new level of intimacy.

In less than a week this woman has imprinted herself onto my very soul, and I'm ready to show the world what she means to me.

"Zara, babe. Wake up." I rub the palm of her hand and she grunts at me, not happy with me waking her at one a.m.

"Fuck off, Jackson," she mumbles in her sleep. I put aside the heart-wrenching realisation that she's dreaming about her brother.

"Babe, you need to wake up. You've been waiting for this."

She drags open her eyes as though it's the hardest thing she's ever had to do.

"Noah?"

"Come on, you need to get out of bed."

She doesn't question why although she does protest as I try to wrap her up warm in her dressing gown and coat to keep her warm against the minus four temperature outside.

"Ugh. It's dark. I can't see a thing. God, I hate you right now." Groggy, grumpy Zara might be my new favourite thing.

I chuckle as I steer her out the door. "You won't in a minute."

"Oh my god," she gasps.

I wish I was recording her reaction because her eyes shoot open the moment we step outside. Green and white hues are dancing across the black sky above us. "Noah," she whispers, looking around in wonderment.

I wrap my arms around her waist from behind, resting my chin on her shoulder and let out a low satisfied rumble as she snuggles into me.

I don't know how long we stand there, watching the sky together in comfortable silence. But I do know it's one of my favourite memories with her. Even though no words have been spoken between us, the communication is clear: we're falling for each other fast. And although it's quick and unexpected, it's right.

Chapter Fourteen

Zara

It's Christmas Eve and the day I've been dreading has arrived.

On our way back to real life, we call into the care home to visit Noah's dad.

"He's doing really well today," the nurse says, leading us through a warren of corridors to the conservatory, which Noah tells me is his dad's favourite spot. "Much better than the last time you saw him."

Noah grips my hand tighter.

I'm shocked to see how frail Noah's dad has gotten over the years, but I do my best to hide it, giving him a brilliant beaming smile instead.

"Hi, Dad." Noah hugs his father. "This is Zara, Jackson McIntosh's sister. Do you remember Zara?"

"I do, it must have been years. Look at you all grown up." He hugs me before holding me at arm's length. His brows pinch together, trying to work out exactly how many years have passed since he last saw me. I'm sure I look older than he would expect me to.

"It's good to see you," I tell him. His smile quickly returns, but it's not hard to see there's something missing.

"Dad, Zara is my girlfriend."

Girlfriend. It's the first time he's called me that and I like it.

His eyes light up like the Christmas tree in the corner as he looks between us. "Ah finally!" he jokes and Noah laughs.

"Let's sit down and have some tea, shall we?" Noah asks, giving me a content smile.

For the next few hours, we drink endless cups of tea and Noah and his dad entertain me with stories of Christmas from Noah's childhood. Thankfully, the walk down memory lane pleases Noah's dad, and we have a wonderful festive afternoon.

"We were just about to take the residents to the bandstand to watch the carollers. Would you like to come?" an older nurse asks us.

"Would that be ok?" Noah asks me, and I nod excitedly.

"I'd love that."

Together with Noah's dad and some of the other residents, we wrap up warm and cross the green that stands between the care home and the bandstand in the centre of the village square.

As we find a comfortable spot to watch, Noah's dad holds out his hands to me. I offer mine in return and we dance to the upbeat jingle of "Jingle Bell Rock" together as Noah watches us with a smile.

"I taught Noah everything he knows about dancing," he tells me.

"It's true, he did. I can show you later." He chuckles, watching us with tears in his eyes.

After an hour or so of dancing and singing along merrily, the care home round up their residents and we wish them all a Merry Christmas.

It's late afternoon when we get to my office and as I suspected, Colin's is the only car in the car park.

"Are you ready? There's no pressure to do this, babe."

"I'm ready. I'm going to go in there, pack up my office, and then tell him I'm quitting. I shouldn't be more than ten minutes."

"And you're sure you don't want me to come in with you?" Noah is reluctant to let me go in alone. But he needn't worry. Colin, although heartless, is completely harmless.

The office is empty when I let myself into the main floor. I thought leaving the job I've worked in for over a decade would be sad and emotional, but it's not. It goes to show how much I've moved on from this world. Packing my things barely takes five minutes. I have a few textbooks, some framed certificates that I take from the wall and my address book with all my local media contacts. I'm clearing my drawer when Colin eventually appears in my doorway.

"Zara. Feeling better I see." His eyes narrow as he watches me pack my things.

"Mmm hmm. Much better."

I don't offer an explanation as to why I called in sick or what I'm doing now. Suddenly the words don't come as easily to me when faced with my ex-husband. *Is that how I lasted so long in that marriage? Because I was too scared to speak up?*

"Are you going somewhere?" He nods to the bag for life propped open on my desk.

"I'm handing in my resignation, effective immediately." I take a deep breath and stand up straighter, trying to muster a shred of confidence to hand him my printed letter. "I'm sorry, Colin, but I can't work for you anymore. After what happened and the breakdown of our marriage, I need to put myself first for once. So, I'm leaving. You don't have to worry about paying me my notice period or anything, I just... I need to go my own way—"

"You can't leave, Zara. Are you fucking insane? The election is in a fortnight. Do you know how that'll look for me? It could lose me my seat in parliament!" His temper shocks me, but it's his expression that terrifies me. He looks unhinged as he takes a menacing step towards me, making my heart race. "Think about it, don't be a foolish girl. If my wife quits right before an election, it'll look like I'm up to no good."

"I have to. I can't work here with you, especially not when your mistress still works here too. I can't do it anymore. I need to have some respect for myself."

My anxiety peaks when he doesn't stop his advances, until he's in my face, blocking my exit from the room. I look around, trying my best not to panic, but unless he moves, I'm trapped.

Fuck, I made a mistake coming here alone.

I was stupid to think I *could* do this on my own.

I should have let Noah come in with me, there's no way I can fight off Colin, he's almost twice my weight. He'll easily overpower me before I have a chance to scream for help.

I think back to that half an hour of self-defence they taught the girls when I started university, but all I can think is don't wear a ponytail as it's easier to grab from behind and always keep my keys in my fist when walking alone at night.

Nothing has prepared me to have to fight off my ex.

"It's Christmas Eve, I need to go. I'll come back for the rest of my things between Christmas and New Year and maybe once you've calmed down, we can talk." I try to sidestep around him, but he grabs my wrist, yanking me to him so hard I yelp in pain as he raises my arm between us.

"You're not leaving," he growls as a panicked sob escapes me.

"Get the fuck off her," Noah roars as he bursts through the office door. He grabs Colin by the scruff of his shirt and yanks him away from me, tossing him onto the ground.

Without giving him a chance to stand by himself, Noah drags him to his feet and pins him against the wall by his throat. Tears spill down my cheeks as I watch Noah threaten him.

"Don't hurt him, Noah. Please. It's not worth it."

"I swear to god, you lay so much as a pinkie finger on her again and I will end you. Do you understand me?"

"I should have fucking guessed she'd bring a guard dog.

She's too weak to face me herself. Always has been, she's got no backbone has my Zara."

"She's not yours," Noah snarls. "Zara, grab what you need and let's go, you're not coming back here."

I rush around the room, hastily grabbing what's left of my possessions and throwing them into my bag, while Noah holds a struggling Colin uncomfortably against the wall.

"Go wait in the car," he orders.

"I'm not leaving you here, Noah. Not alone with him."

Although physically Noah is the bigger threat, Colin has friends in high places, mainly the police force. If Noah laid a finger on him, he'd be done for.

"She might not belong to me anymore, but she'll never belong to you either," Colin says when Noah finally lets him go. "As soon as her parents find out about this, they'll make sure we get back together. It's only a matter of time."

"That's where you're wrong, mate. Because this past week while Zara has been calling in sick to you, she's been in my bed with me." He strolls over to me, guiding me out of the office with an arm placed protectively on my lower back.

"Thank you for looking out for me," I whisper when we're in the safety of his truck.

"I'll always look out for you," he tells me, taking my trembling hand as he reaches over the centre console and bringing it up to his lips so he can kiss my knuckles. I lean over and kiss him, not caring that we could be seen, I need to show him how thankful I am he's here.

He pulls out of the kiss first, leaning his forehead against mine.

"I know we've spent the past week in each other's pockets, but could you stay with me tonight? I don't... I don't want to be alone."

He kisses my forehead softly.

"Of course, I'll stay. I'll stay for as long as you need me to."

Chapter Fifteen

Noah

Zara has been quiet since the run-in with Colin. Every now and then I'll catch her twirling her wrist or absentmindedly rubbing the skin there and it bothers me. I hate that I let that happen to her. I hate that I wasn't there to protect her the second he turned on her.

"Does it hurt?" I ask guiltily, looking over my shoulder to where she still sits at the kitchen table. I'm washing up the last of the dishes from dinner and although I'm facing the sink, I can feel the stress rolling off her in waves.

"No, it doesn't hurt. Not physically anyway. I never thought he'd ever lay a hand on me."

I dry my hands on a towel, bend down in front of her and gently take her hands in mine, inspecting her wrist closely. It's not red anymore thankfully, and she said it doesn't hurt, but I still want to be sure.

"Babe, I'm sorry. I should have come in with you from the start."

"I made you stay in the car, it's not your fault."

"It's not yours either. From now on, if you need to see him, I promise I'll be right there with you. You don't have to see him alone."

She gives me a sorry smile. "I feel like the worst person. I hate that I ruined your Christmas Eve."

"You didn't. We had a wonderful afternoon with my dad and seeing you with him, seeing him smiling and laughing as he danced with you, it made my Christmas. It's a memory I'll cherish forever. Besides, it's only eight o'clock, there's still plenty of time to enjoy Christmas Eve together."

"That reminds me, your dad said he taught you everything you know about dancing. You kept that quiet..."

I groan. "Because I'm terrible at dancing. Unlike Dad, I lack rhythm."

"Oh, come on! Let's dance. We can start a new Christmas Eve tradition." She looks at me with her wide eyes full of excitement, and I can't say no to her. "No one is here to see us, it doesn't matter that we're rubbish."

"For you, anything."

I rise to my feet and pull out my phone, selecting a romantic Michael Bublé song.

"Zara McIntosh, may I have this dance?" I bend forward, offering her my hand while the other stays behind my back like we're in some Christmas movie where the princess falls in love with a pauper. She takes it immediately and I pull her so her body is flush with mine.

"You really have made my Christmas, Zara."

"And you've made mine too."

We sway together in her kitchen until the very last song on the album finishes playing and even then, I'm not ready to let go.

***

Zara

I wake the next day in my own bed, tucked into Noah's side as he nuzzles into me. I'm glad to see nothing has changed since we've been home. He didn't give it a second thought when I asked him to stay with me. Even if I hadn't asked him, I get the feeling he would have insisted anyway.

"Good morning," I say, my voice still groggy and tired when he stirs next to me.

"Merry Christmas, beautiful."

My heart feels so full when he looks at me. I know we're only a week into this romance but truthfully, I can feel myself falling for him. And the quickness of it doesn't even scare me.

"Merry Christmas." I kiss him, letting out a content sigh as I do. "What time are you meeting Jackson?"

"Not until eleven. I was hoping we could have a chilled-out Christmas morning together until then. If you'd like to that is."

"That sounds perfect." I roll onto my back, stretching out my spine with a yawn.

"Out of all the sounds you make in bed with me, I think that one is my favourite."

"What?" I ask incredulously.

"You sound like a baby dinosaur," he explains, and laughter erupts out of me. "It's adorable."

His smile fades as he watches me rub my eyes. Noah turns onto his side, tucking an arm beneath his head, propping himself up slightly to face me.

"Everything ok?" I ask, mirroring him and shifting myself closer so our naked bodies are entwined.

"How do you think your parents are going to react?" Worry swims in his eyes.

"Honestly, I have no idea. I hope they'll see how happy I am since Colin and I separated. I hope they'll see how happy I am with you. But if I'm being honest with myself, I'm worried they won't approve of my choice to leave him. Dad has had many public affairs and Mam has always turned a blind eye, pretending it doesn't bother her." I look down at his chest rising and falling, finding comfort in him being here. "I guess I'm preparing myself for disappointment."

"I wish I could tell you it's all going to be okay…but either way, I'll be there for you, whatever you need."

"Right now, I don't want to think about it. There's no use stressing, I just want to enjoy the morning with my boyfriend."

He grins at me, rolling me onto my back and caging me in with his arms.

"Really? And what did you have in mind?" he asks, his dick already springing to life between us.

"I thought we could have some breakfast and spend the

morning in bed?"

"Sounds perfect, babe. Because I was thinking I might have my breakfast in bed."

He kisses down my neck, reaching my naked breasts and pulling a nipple into his mouth.

"I think that's a great idea," I moan as he nudges my thighs apart and discovers just how desperate I am for him.

When he disappears under the covers, I lie back and let all my thoughts vanish, every last thought but Noah.

Chapter Sixteen

Noah

At eleven a.m., I'm waiting at the local pub with two pints of lager in front of me. One for me and one for Jackson. Families have started to arrive for their Christmas dinner and as the place gets busier, the more anxious I get.

Everyone is so festive and excited. Christmas music rings through the air and the smell of roast meats drift into the bar from the kitchen, but I'm struggling to find the positives in the atmosphere.

By eleven thirty, Jackson still hasn't arrived, and I've almost finished my drink alone when I get a text.

Jackson: Won't make the pub today, I've been called into the office.

Great. Of course, he has. On Christmas fucking Day of all days. I don't think it's a difficult request to meet him today when he's supposed to be at his parents' at twelve for dinner anyway, but clearly, work is more important to him than having this conversation with me.

"Hey, how'd he take it?" Zara asks when she answers my call on the first ring.

"He didn't show. He sent a text two minutes ago saying he had to go into the office for something."

"On Christmas Day?" Her disbelief echoes my own.

"Apparently so." I shrug.

"I'm so sorry. He's such a prick." I try to smile and lighten my mood a little, but the truth is, I'm really disappointed in my friend. "I'm about five minutes away from the pub. Meet me outside and we'll walk the rest of the way together."

"Okay, I'll see you soon, babe." I hang up and drain the rest of my pint, leaving Jackson's untouched. I pull on my coat, carry the glasses back to the bar and wish the staff a merry Christmas before I brave the cold outside.

Zara appears around the corner a moment later, dressed in a little black dress, black tights and a pillar-box red coat with a black faux fur collar, looking the epitome of Christmas.

"Hey," she says, her smile lightening my mood. She keeps a respectable distance between us, and I hate that I can't touch her because even though my dad and Colin know about our relationship, we decided to still keep our distance in public until we tell Zara's family over dinner.

At least that was the plan until Jackson bailed on me.

"Hey," I say, my smile coming easier now that she's here. "Let me carry that." I take the small bag of gifts from her as we continue the short walk to her parents' together.

"Thank you." She smiles as our fingers brush, an intentional move on my part.

Zara's anxiety is palpable, gaining in intensity the closer we get to her parents' bungalow the next street over. I wish I knew what's going through her head, I wish I knew how to make everything better for her with a click of my fingers.

"It's going to be okay," she tells me, probably sensing my own anxieties. "I know you wanted to tell Jackson separately, but we can play by ear when he gets here."

"I know, you're right."

Fuck it, I reach over and squeeze her hand.

Zara reaches for the door handle. A sound from behind us gets our attention so I let go of her hand. I turn expecting to see Jackson climbing out of a taxi that's pulled up at the kerb, but instead, rage surges through me at the sight of Colin.

"Zara, baby." He jogs up to us, smiles and kisses her on the cheek.

"Oh my god," she says, alarm radiating from her. She doesn't step away, too frozen to move an inch.

"What did I say about touching her," I growl, stepping closer to him, my hands balling into fists at my side as I barely hang on to my senses.

"Nice to see you, Noah." He extends his hand to me, but I bat it away with the back of mine.

"Oh, you're here," Janet, Zara's mam, says excitedly, appearing in the doorway completely oblivious to the exchange happening in her front garden.

It's hard, but I stand down, not knowing what to do for the best right now. It's not my place to spill everything, no matter how badly I want to punch Colin in the face.

"Colin dear, you got here right on time. Can you help Stuart with the fire in the sunroom? He's struggling. And hello, my darling, Merry Christmas!" Her mam comes to hug and kiss her. I glare at Colin, a silent threat letting him know I won't take this lying down, no matter how helpless I feel inside. "Come on in, you must be freezing. What were you doing out here in the snow? You know the door is always open." Oblivious to the tension coming from Zara and me, her mam fusses us inside. "Noah, lovely to see you, sweetheart. Merry Christmas." She kisses me once on each cheek. "Zara, take Noah's coat please and pop it in the back bedroom with yours and Colin's."

"Okay." Zara is pale, her eyes lifeless as she takes my coat and leaves without another word. Her mam doesn't seem to notice anything is wrong with her daughter and that kills me. It also extinguishes any hope I had that they'd be happy for me and Zara.

"I'm going to pop to the loo, if that's okay?" I say, searching for an excuse to follow her down the corridor.

"Of course, you know where it is, you don't need to ask." She smiles at me kindly and makes her way into the main body of the bungalow. It doesn't warm me like it used to, now that I see her in a completely different light.

Once she's gone, I dart from the room, following Zara's footsteps, hoping to find her in one of the bedrooms. In all the years

I've been coming here for Christmas dinner, not once has Colin been here, despite being part of their family, always choosing to spend the day at his parents' house instead.

After searching a couple of bedrooms, I find Zara in the bathroom, sitting on the edge of the bath with her head in her hands close to hyperventilating. Her hands are trembling and her shoulders shudder as she tries to catch her breath.

"Zara, babe. It's going to be okay." I try my best to calm her with soothing circles on her back. "That's it. Keep breathing."

"Merry Christmas!" another voice calls from the hallway.

Zara's face morphs from pale grey to sickly green. I have no idea what to do here. Everything that could go wrong today seems to be happening and I'm powerless to stop it.

"Oh my god," she whispers, tears brimming her eyes. "It's his parents."

Anger and frustration surge through me in a protective wave. She doesn't deserve to feel this way in her own parents' house. As much as I want to go out there and give Colin a piece of my mind for letting this spiral, I choose Zara instead because she needs me.

"Tell me what you need." I crouch in front of her, holding onto both trembling hands.

"Please don't leave me alone with him," her voice breaks into a silent sob.

"I promise. Okay, I'm here. I'll be right by your side the whole day. No matter what."

I pluck off a piece of toilet tissue and dab her eyes, picking up the stray tears that have started to fall.

"I hate that he's doing this. Why can't he leave me be?"

"Because he can see you're happy, he can see that you're stronger without him, and he hates it."

I pull her into my arms, holding her tightly trying to make her feel safe.

"We can't tell them today, can we?" she asks, looking up at me.

"We can tell them tomorrow or the day after, whenever you want to." I brush her hair back from her face, neatly placing it behind her ear where it was before her panic attack. "For now, let's get through dinner."

She nods. "I can do this."

"I know you can." I give her a reassuring smile, check her make-up is intact and together we sneak out of the bathroom and into the sunroom where everyone is gathered, including Jackson, who has a face like thunder when he sees us enter together.

Chapter Seventeen

Zara

Christmas dinner is, to be brutally honest, a fucking shit show.

The air is thick with tension. I'm pissed off with Colin. Noah is pissed off with Jackson and for some reason Jackson is pissed off with all of us.

Just like my and Colin's parents, Jackson's girlfriend, Nikole, is oblivious to anything that doesn't involve her, so she's chatting nicely with Colin as though they're long-time besties.

My eyes flit from person to person, struggling to keep calm after my panic attack in the bathroom earlier. My anxiety is through the roof, and I can already feel the hives spreading over my chest.

We all continue to eat in an extremely uncomfortable silence until Dad, bless him, tries to start a conversation with me.

"How was your time away, Zara?" Dad asks innocently. My cutlery squeaks against my plate.

"You've been away?" Jackson asks me, putting his own cutlery down on the table and folding his arms across his chest. He looks at me with a stern, unfamiliar expression I've not seen on my brother before. "Both of you?" He looks at Colin for confirmation.

"I was at work, unfortunately," Colin answers. "I would have loved to have gone with her, but I couldn't get away with the election being so close."

"It's not like you to take a holiday at such a crucial time," Dad says with a disapproving head shake. I see Noah's jaw tighten as he tries his best to keep his cool.

"She works hard, don't you, baby?" Colin coos, taking my hand on top of the table. "She deserves a break."

"Where did you go?" Jackson probes further. *What the fuck is his problem?!*

"I went to a little cabin in Kielder." I've never been able to lie to my brother, so I hope omitting some truths saves me. "I needed time away to relax and recuperate from the busy year."

"Huh... Interesting." He glares at Noah this time. That's when it hits me.

It's pointless lying to my brother at all because he knows who I was really with. But there's no way he can know the full truth and that's what scares me most.

Unable to take any more, Noah stands from the table.

"Jackson, can I have a word in the kitchen." He says it as a statement rather than a question. My brother scrapes his chair back, glowering at me and following Noah out of the room.

"I need a drink," I announce to the table. I spring up and follow, leaving behind confused murmurings I pay no attention to.

"Jackson!" I plead as I jog up to him, grasping at his arm, doing my best to pull him back. I need him to listen to me before he makes a mistake he can't take back. "Jackson, I can explain everything. It's not what you think and it's definitely not what it looks like."

The moment the kitchen door swings closed behind the three of us, his fist is flying through the air, connecting with Noah's face with a crunch. The sound of Noah's nose breaking makes me sick to the stomach. And then comes the blood.

"Ah fuck!" Noah doubles over not even bothering to fight back against his best friend.

"You just can't stay away, can you? Do you think I don't see the way you've been looking at her lately? Do you think I've been totally fucking oblivious?" Jackson spits out, keeping his voice low. "What I can't understand though, is why you felt you needed to play games with my sister's life and ruin her marriage!"

"What are you talking about, you fucking psychopath!" I yell at my brother, losing my cool completely as I run to Noah's side, throwing my arm around his shoulder as he's doubled over. "Noah, oh my god, are you okay?"

Blood is pouring from his nose, dripping and forming a puddle on the white kitchen tiles. I dash across the kitchen as quickly as I can and pull a clean tea towel from the drawer. I do my best to stop the blood pouring from Noah's broken face, but it flows quickly.

"How could you be so naive, Zara? You could lose everything!"

"You're a fucking arsehole, Jackson. Quick to judge and act before you even know all the facts." I shove at my brother's chest as Noah collapses into a chair, clutching the towel to his nose.

"I know exactly what's going on," he yells in a whisper as though we haven't already been heard by the entire street let alone the next room. He pulls up some photos on his phone and turns it so I can see. "I've paid a lot of money to have these buried, so you better have a really good explanation."

I take the phone from him, swiping through the pictures quickly. There's one of me and Noah outside of Chateaux Minx where he's carrying me in his arms to his truck. Another, from when we'd gotten back to my house, and he told me he had feelings for me as we stood on my garden path. Next, there's one from the next morning when he picked me up with my suitcase. There are dozens more of them, all seem to have been taken with a long-lens camera capturing what does look like an affair.

I don't know how this person knew to follow me, or if they've been following me for a while and this is the first sniff they've gotten of a scandal, but either way, I feel like I might throw up.

And then I look at Jackson and I'm not sure if I'm more hurt by the stalker or the fact my own brother believes that I would have an affair, let alone blame Noah for it. Noah is his best friend in the world, and he turned on him in a split second.

"WHAT ON EARTH IS GOING ON IN HERE?!" Mam screams the second she walks into the kitchen and sees Noah's bloody face, the rest of our guests filling in after her.

I look at each of them one by one, wondering how on earth I'm going to get out of this one and still protect everyone in this room.

The truth is, I can't protect everyone. So, I choose the person who matters most. I choose to tell the truth and protect myself.

"Jackson punched Noah because he thought we were having an affair. Truth is…Colin and I separated six months ago," I say, glaring at Jackson from my spot next to Noah.

"What!?" my dad booms.

My mam gasps dramatically and I swear, Colin's mam actually clutches the string of pearls around her neck.

"Zara," Colin warns me with a threatening tone to his voice, and I feel the shift in the room immediately. Jackson goes from glaring at Noah to Colin, having finally accepted he got the wrong end of the stick.

"Oh my god, this is terrible." Mam starts to cry about our family reputation and some other superficial shit, and honestly, I should have expected it. Oh, how I've brought shame on the family name by getting divorced.

"Why?" Jackson keeps his eyes trained on my ex-husband, but the question is for me. I'm the only one who will tell the truth; I can already see Colin trying to string together a web of lies in his head.

"Colin cheated on me with my assistant. He's been living with his mistress ever since I caught them red-handed. It wasn't the first affair…I later found out there have been multiple women over the course of our marriage, maybe even longer than that."

Colin's mam joins in the crying, hugging onto my own mum for support. "Surely, it's not too late. You can work it out, I'm sure. Worse things have happened, there's no need to make rash decisions like getting a divorce."

"I told you, Zara, we can work it out. I apologised to you with all my heart. I'm committed to making this work. We can try therapy and counselling." Colin bats his eyelashes innocently.

Noah audibly groans when Colin starts getting *emotional*.

"I know a great marriage counsellor," his mam offers.

"Oh, is it Dr Jenkins? We used him and he was wonderful," Mam adds, and the matriarchs continue their praise of this miracle therapist.

I can't take it anymore.

I absolutely fucking lose it because I can't take any more of their shit.

"Are you listening to me?! Why would I want to work things out with a man who clearly has no respect for me? Why should I stay in a loveless marriage? To save face or protect the family name from scandal? If I want the world to respect me, I need to respect myself, so for the first time I'm putting myself first. Colin, you're a fuckhead, I wouldn't get back with you even if you told me you could shit gold bullion."

Mam tries to protest, but I cut her off.

"You walked in here seeing that your son punched his best friend in the face. There's blood on the floor and Noah is clutching a towel to his face. You haven't even bothered to check he's okay. You're more bothered about your reputation." I place my palm on his shoulder, and he places his hand over mine in a show of solidarity.

Mam looks at Noah as if she's realising for the first time what's really going on. Dad doesn't say a word; he's so red in the face I worry he's going to pass out.

"So, you aren't having an affair...but you are together?" Jackson asks.

"Our relationship is new, but in the short time we've been together he's shown me more love, affection, respect, and support than I thought possible. The list is endless, and what does he get for it? A fist to the face from my idiot brother who got the wrong end of the stick."

"Zara, I'm so sorry." My brother takes a step closer to me and Noah but since I'm on a roll, I let him have it too.

"Don't you start with me, Jackson, because I've had it with your shit. You used to be my best friend. You're my big brother and I looked up to you. I used to be able to count on you. But where have you been for the past six months when I've needed you? You've been a shitty brother and a shitty friend too because not only have you let me down when I needed you, you let him down too." I turn away from him to Noah, who despite having a tea towel gripped against his bleeding face still smiles at me. "You've got some nerve coming in here throwing your fists around as though you're a protective big brother. Come on, Noah, let's get you to the hospital." The bleeding hasn't stopped and I'm starting to get worried.

When he stands, he pulls me in close, leaning his arm around my shoulder so I can guide him out of the room with one arm around his back and the other on his stomach.

I ignore everyone else in the room, focusing on the only person that matters to me right now.

"I'm so proud of you." His words are muffled but I hear them, nonetheless.

"I'm proud of me too," I say, the realisation of what I've done almost crushing me. If it wasn't for Noah whimpering in pain when I accidentally walk him into the hallway wall, I think I'd have passed out by now.

"Wait, Zara! Noah!" My brother calls after us, catching up to us at the front door.

"Fuck off, Jackson, you've caused enough trouble tonight," I say through gritted teeth.

"Please, I'm sorry. Let me drive you to the hospital."

"And why should I? You're the reason we're going to the hospital in the first place!"

As much as I want to hate him right now, I'm also aware that we need him. We walked here today, and I don't think I could manage the walk back to my house to get my car when Noah is struggling with the pain.

"Here's my keys, get him in, I'll get all of our stuff."

"It's fine, let him come," Noah says, seeing the conflict in my eyes.

"Fine." I snatch the keys from my brother's grasp. "But only because I have no other choice. If it were up to me, I'd tell you to go to hell."

Chapter Eighteen

Noah

The drive to the hospital, although short, is fucking awkward just like dinner.

Jackson drives with me and Zara in the back of his sleek silver Mercedes, and he never once complains about blood stains on his upholstery, which is very unlike Jackson, so I assume the guilt is getting to him. I know Jackson is sorry. He reacted without thinking and I saw the gut-wrenching reaction he had when Zara yelled at him, putting him in his place.

It's like she slapped him across the face, which come to think of it, wouldn't have hurt as much as my face is fucking killing right now.

All eyes are on us as we walk into the hospital waiting room. It's not every day a prize-winning political journalist and the beloved wife of the local MP drag their blood-soaked friend into A&E.

Saying it like that sounds like the start of a really bad joke.

We join the long line at reception, ignoring the staring.

"Noah Williams…" Zara tells the woman behind the glass.

Her eyes land on mine immediately and she types in my name into her computer. "My brother punched him in the face because he's a fucking psych—"

"It was a misunderstanding. We're fine," I jump in. If they call the police, Zara will freak out. If Jackson got arrested, despite the reason, she'd be devastated. "I've got a broken nose."

The receptionist takes the rest of my details as if she sees this a thousand times a day, reaches into a fridge below her desk to pass me an ice pack and points us back towards the packed waiting room where I sit between the feuding siblings.

Zara snuggles into my side, linking her arm through mine, not caring that we're in public, at the very hospital named after her ex-husband's family ironically enough.

Initially, I thought the waiting time on the screen of six hours was an exaggeration but finally, not long after seven p.m., we're called into a side room where I finally get to lie back on a bed and rest my aching face.

"A doctor will be with you shortly," the nurse tells us with a smile before closing the door behind her.

"I'm really sorry, mate," Jackson says as I groan in agony again, and Zara makes a scoffing noise like she has every time he's apologised since we got here.

"Babe, do you think you can get me a cup of water or something from the fountain please?"

She looks at me and I can tell she's considering arguing that she needs to be in on the conversation I'm about to have with her brother but finally she relents.

"I swear to god, Jackson, if a single hair on his head is out of place when I get back, I will murder you, slowly and painfully."

"I promise," he says, looking genuinely terrified of her, and so he should, because her threat is very real.

She leans over and kisses my shoulder before she walks out of the room with a disgruntled sigh.

"Is it bad?" I ask, finally taking away the ice pack now that Zara isn't here to see the extent of the damage. I wouldn't be surprised if my nose is facing sideways, at least that's how it feels.

Jackson winces when he looks at me, so I take that as a yes.

"I was going to tell you about Zara today that's why I asked you to meet me before lunch. We planned to tell your family at dinner and wanted your support first. If you hadn't guessed, we expected them to protest. We could have done with you being on our side," I tell him. "But then you didn't show and everything turned into a huge cluster-fuck with Colin and his psycho parents showing up."

"I was paying to get those images destroyed. They said I had until two p.m. today or they'd be released in the evening paper. I didn't believe it at first but when I saw them, I jumped to the wrong conclusion."

"Why did you pay for them when you thought we were having an affair? If you were so pissed off at us, why help us?"

"Because I'd do anything to protect my sister. You know that."

"Like burying a body or bailing her out of jail if she needed it?" I ask with a laugh.

"Exactly."

"I get it, I'd do the same for her too."

"You really care about her, don't you?" He tilts his head to the side, looking at me with a curious expression. "You've never expressed any attraction to her, you've never mentioned wanting a relationship with anyone, never mind Zara. I saw a change in the way you were looking at her, but I didn't think it was serious feelings."

"I started having feelings for her at your birthday party. I didn't know it at the time, but it was the day she kicked Colin out. Then the moment we got together I felt like I was exactly where I'm meant to be."

"Do I want to know the specifics of how you got together?" He cringes, already regretting asking.

"Absolutely not." I laugh.

"Gross." He laughs too and I'm so happy to hear the sound.

"All you need to know as her brother is that I make her happy and I'll make it my mission to make her happy for the rest of my life or for however long she'll keep me. I'm falling for her, Jackson. I'm falling in love with her hard and fast and nothing is going to stop it."

Zara walks back into the room, holding a small cup of water and wearing the biggest grin on her face.

"You heard all that, didn't you?"

She nods, her smile widening as she lets out a laugh mixed

with an emotional sob. "The water machine is right outside, and the doors are thin." Tears of happiness shine in her eyes as she crosses the room. "I'm falling for you too."

The bed dips slightly as she sits on the edge, leaning down to kiss me on the cheek, and despite the sharp stabbing pain in my face, I turn and kiss her on the mouth.

"Okay, this is going to take some getting used to." Her brother groans when she kisses me back.

"He might have forgiven you, and yes, I appreciate what you did to get rid of those pictures, but mark my words, you've still got some grovelling to do. It doesn't excuse your shitty behaviour at all." Her words are menacing so I give her a pleading look. "He broke your face, Noah! That's my second favourite part of your body." She smirks and I know that was added to make her brother uncomfortable.

"Okay, nope." Jackson holds his hands up in surrender. "I'll wait in the hallway."

I laugh as my best friend runs out of the room before she opens her mouth again.

"So, you're falling for me?" I ask, stroking her hair back so I can look her in the eyes.

"Noah Williams, I think I already have."

"Me too." I grin, happiness oozing out of me. She snuggles into my side as we wait for the doctor and although this is only the beginning of sorting out the mess from today, it feels great to finally have someone else on our side.

Epilogue – One Year Later

Zara

I'll never get bored of watching Noah chop wood at the cottage. The taut muscles in his tanned forearms strain as he lowers the axe, splitting the thickest log I've ever seen clean in half. That piece of wood didn't stand a chance, much like me.

"Can you please stop staring at him like he's a piece of meat?" Jackson groans with an extravagant eye roll, cutting through the beginnings of a very naughty daydream about the time I had him bend me over that old wood-chopping tree stump back in the summer. "I might be fine with you two being together, but I'd rather not see your thirstiness first-hand."

"Thirstiness?" I look at my brother with raised eyebrows. He sits at the table in the open-plan kitchen living area of the cottage, steaming hot coffee in hand.

"It's what the kids say these days."

"You're a thirty-five-year-old man, Jackson. Not a kid," I tease, taking a seat next to him, rubbing my growing stomach. Although there's three months left until baby girl's due date, I feel like a house end.

"You need to brush up on the lingo if you're going to be a parent." He jokes, but there's something missing from his smile, something that's been missing for a long time now.

In the past year, Jackson has made more of an effort to see me and Noah, and since we got pregnant and moved in together, we try to have him over for a meal at least once a month.

"Are you okay?" I ask, looking at my big brother. He's looking stressed but lately, I've put that down to his impending New Year's Eve nuptials to Nikole. It's the wedding of the year, according to OK magazine, celebrities and billionaires galore. I'd be lying if I said I was looking forward to it.

"You've had a tough year, what with Noah's dad passing away and then Mam and Dad being dicks again." I laugh at his candidness. "Was it all worth it?"

I smile at my bump with so much love I didn't know I was capable of.

Surprisingly, my parents didn't take that long to come around to the idea of having a divorcee for a daughter. But when I told them I was moving in with Noah out of wedlock and having his baby, it was Christmas Day all over again. It's not entirely their fault. They both grew up in a world where you did things in a certain order and women had a certain role in a household. And for the longest time that was me too, but now, after seeing how good life can be with a partner who loves and respects me, I'm determined to break that cycle for our children.

When Mam and Dad saw the scan picture for the first time, they immediately fell in love.

"It was." We may have had a challenging year, but I'd do it all again if I had to.

"Do you think you'll ever marry Noah?"

"We've talked about it and yeah, we will get married eventually. We're in no rush, but I do want to share Noah's surname with him and our daughter."

"You never took Colin's surname," he observes thoughtfully.

"Yeah, in hindsight there were many reg flags our marriage was never going to last." I watch my brother carefully. "Jackson, what's going on here?"

"How did you know that Noah was the right person?"

"Because when Noah and I got together, my life felt like it was finally falling into place. It was the craziest thing because everything just made sense. I thought what I had with Colin was normal because it's all I'd ever known, but it wasn't, and I didn't know that until Noah showed me what it really meant to be loved." Noah chooses this moment to enter the room again, tossing aside his flannel shirt, leaving him in a grey sweat-soaked T-shirt. He bends down, placing a hand on my stomach which the baby kicks happily, and gives me a chaste kiss on the lips. "He showed me what it meant to be happy. So yeah, it might not have been easy, but it's all been worth it," I finish.

Jackson doesn't say anything else, he doesn't ask any more questions, instead he looks out of the window at the snow-covered hills in the distance in a contemplative silence.

"Are you happy, Jackson?" I ask, exchanging worried glances with Noah.

"I will be." He stands abruptly and drains his cup, wincing as the liquid burns his throat. "I'll see you tomorrow at Mam's for Christmas dinner."

And with that, he's gone.

"What was that about?" Noah asks.

"I have no idea."

***

Noah

As planned, Zara and I make our way to her parents' house on Christmas Day after spending the morning in our cabin wrapped up in each other. We've been spending more and more time there since Dad died. I had Wi-Fi put in so Zara can run her PR company from the smallest spare room, while I've decorated the other for our daughter.

I smile over at Zara, sitting in the passenger seat rubbing her bump affectionately; my entire world in one frame.

"You're still worried about Jackson, aren't you?" I ask as she gnaws on her lower lip.

"Yeah." She sighs.

"I'm sure it's just a little pre-wedding nerves. I'll talk to him today, see if I can get him to open up to me." I reach for her hand, squeezing it affectionately.

Janet is waiting in the freezing cold for us when we arrive, a big grin splitting her face when she spots her pregnant daughter.

"Merry Christmas." She smiles, giving Zara a tight hug and ushering us into the hallway where her dad waits. When I take Zara's coat, her mam coos at her stomach. "May I?"

"Go ahead." Zara chuckles, giving her permission to touch her bump.

Janet gasps, placing a second hand on her. "Did you feel that? She kicked!" Tears well up in her eyes as Zara's dad pushes her aside to get a feel too, before shaking my hand firmly.

"Jackson's in the living room," he tells me, and Zara and I go off to find her brother, anxious to see what version of him we'll find today, the grumpy distant one or the anxious mess he seemed to be yesterday.

"No Nikole?" I ask when we find my best friend in the living room alone, sitting in an armchair by the huge Christmas tree.

"No," he says with an excited grin. He doesn't offer any explanation as to where his bride-to-be is, which is even odder. "This is nice, isn't it. It's like old times. Just the three of us hanging out."

Zara takes a seat on the sofa next to the window, opening it wide. "Seriously, who put the fire on when it's already so hot," she complains, shedding the rest of her layers until all she wears is a thin T-shirt dress.

"Babe, it's just you that's hot. It was minus four when we woke up this morning and it's not much better now."

"You say that as though I'm not carrying a bowling-ball-sized furnace in my body at all times," she says sarcastically.

"Here, this will cool you down." Jackson is giddy when he hands over a glass of champagne to me and sparkling apple juice with added ice cubes to Zara before settling back into his chair.

Is he drunk already? It's barely lunchtime.

Zara's face is a picture as she stares at him like he's grown an extra head.

I don't have time to probe him about his personality transplant before our dinner is served and we're all called to the dining room. As a family, we talk and laugh as we eat together before returning to the living room to open gifts.

It's like the old Jackson is back. He's relaxed, happy and…looks ten years younger, almost? Like whatever stress has been ageing him lately doesn't exist anymore.

"Okay," Zara's dad says when we're finished with gifts. Placing his arms around his wife's shoulders as they stand in the centre of the living room, he looks at each of us lovingly. "I'd like to raise a toast to our family. We've weathered many storms over the years, and we always come out stronger having learned tough lessons. I know we haven't always set the best example for you kids, but we're committed to setting a better example for our granddaughter and all future grandchildren."

"Hint hint, Jackson." Janet winks and Jackson prematurely drains his champagne flute before the end of the speech, topping it up once more.

"We love you kids so much, and although Noah isn't

officially family on paper, he's family nonetheless and always has been. We're going to spend a long time proving to you how much you all mean to us. Merry Christmas."

Zara cuddles into my side, her head resting on my shoulder as we all echo his sentiments with a loud chorus of "Merry Christmas!"

I place a delicate kiss on her forehead as she closes her eyes. I'm glad to see Zara comfortable with her family again, if not on better terms with them now than she's ever been.

Janet's phone rings, interrupting the moment of celebration.

"Who could that be," she says, pulling on her glasses and picking her phone up from the side table. "Oh, it's Nikole's mother. I wonder what she wants."

"Uh, don't answer that, Mam, I think we need to talk," Jackson blurts out, but it's too late, she's answering the phone call and walking out of the room.

"Congratulations," Jackson says to Zara and me, taking on a sickly green colour and raising to his feet. "You are officially no longer the disappointment of the family."

A perfectly timed, high-pitched scream comes from the next room and Jackson darts out, closing the door behind him.

"Jackson McIntosh! What did you do?!" Janet's voice echoes around the house followed by mumblings from Jackson I can't quite make out.

Zara's dad sighs in resignation, getting to his feet to

investigate.

"Do you think we'll ever have a Christmas Day together without drama?" I ask Zara, settling back into the couch and tugging her closer again.

"I doubt it, but we've got a lifetime of Christmas Days to come," she says, leaning up to kiss me. "We can try again next year."

THE END.

Need more? Want to see how Jackson redeems himself? Pre-order **The Romance Retreat** coming 31st July 2024.

Jackson McIntosh is desperate for an escape, so when an opportunity presents itself to attend what he believes is an exclusive romance writing retreat, he grabs it no questions asked and heads to the Lake District.

Taylor Harrison needs a miracle to save her family's B&B so when a nearby hotel double books a romance retreat, she steps in to save the day hoping it'll save her in return.

Taylor is surprised when the man who jilted her at the altar twelve months ago arrives as a guest with his new girlfriend. Luckily, she has a sexy, brooding writer ready to step in as her fake boyfriend.

One romance retreat, two unlikely singletons with undeniable chemistry thrown in at the deep end, and secrets that could ruin everything... What's the worst that can happen?

Coming Next

A Wearside Story

A football romance series with a difference.

Playing For You

A prequel to the Wearside Story series.

Coming in February 2024

Natasha Borthwick is Wearside FC's Number One, but after an embarrassing string of losses, she's not so sure she deserves that title anymore.

Luke Ramshaw is the hottest developer in the gaming industry but as his deadline to complete his funding application fast approaches, he still has no game demo to present.

The pair are thrown together by a meddling mutual connection in a last-ditch attempt to save both Natasha's team and Luke's career. The problem? They didn't exactly get off to a great start, but what happens when they get closer is a whole other ball game.

https://mybook.to/PlayingForYou

Playing For Real

Book 2 in the Wearside Story series.

Coming 25th April 2024 and available to pre-order now.

Aaron Milburn is one scandal away from losing out on the newly vacated captaincy at Wearside FC.

A Romance For Christmas

The captain of the women's team, Brooke Davison, is done with feeling like a side character in her own story.

When Aaron needs a little help with his ruined reputation, his long-time best friend agrees to be his fake girlfriend. Although, the couple soon learn it's hard to fake it with someone you've fallen in love with.

https://mybook.to/PlayingForReal

Also by Ellie White

Love and London
8 Years ago.

Maggie's life was just as she had planned... Perfect. She had graduated Uni with Honours, had landed her dream job and was married to her childhood sweetheart. One thing that wasn't part of the plan was becoming a widow the night before her 22nd Birthday.

Present time.

Turning 30 has forced Maggie to start asking the difficult questions in life. Should she start using anti-ageing eye cream? How much money should she be paying into her private pension fund each month? Is she finally ready to start dating again?

When Maggie's Dad and his business partner Ray decide to retire early it's up to Maggie and Jake, Ray's arrogant and egotistical son, to take control.

Encouraged by her family and friends, Maggie embarks on an emotional journey of healing and self-discovery as she takes on new challenges, pushes herself from her comfort zone and finds herself on a string of terrible blind dates. All the while Jake tries his best to prove to Maggie that after years of antagonising her, he's not as obnoxious as he has had her believe.

Love in the Wings

Harriet Adams was a West End rising star until a lapse in judgement cost her her dream job, her boyfriend and so called friends.

She packs up her life and moves back to Sunderland where she gets a rare second chance at a career she thrives in. As she's about open a shiny new musical in front of a home audience, she vows that this time, nothing is going to get in her way. With everything riding on this, she'll play it safe, work hard and most importantly, stay away from theatre guys.

Cue Liam Wright, Assistant Stage Manager.

Liam is everything Harriet didn't know she needed in her life, but he also has a secret. One that could advance his own career if he cashes it in. The only catch? It would ruin any chance of happiness with Harriet if she finds out.

Harriet and Liam share a love like no other, but will that be enough to save their budding relationship when the time comes?

https://mybook.to/B0B2H95LJQ

A Romance For Christmas
A Wearside Story
A football romance series with a difference.

Playing For Her
Book 1 in the Wearside Story series

A tragic injury forces footballing legend Molly Davison into early
retirement. Football is her life and now that she can't play anymore, she
embarks on a new path as a coach for Wearside FC.
Captain of the team, Jordan Robinson, is preparing to hang up his boots
at the end of the season and after being in the game his entire life, he's
having an existential crisis. Not to mention the only woman he's ever had
feelings for is back on Wearside, worse still, she's officially off limits.
Molly is Jordan's new coach, she's building a reputation for herself in the
men's game and paving the way for women just like her. Staying away
from the team captain should be a no brainer but when their chemistry
sizzles on and off the pitch, it's easier said than done.
A romance that was once so easy has new challenges as the pair try to
navigate their budding relationship through the world of men's
professional football. Will their love risk the reputation Molly has
worked so hard to build or can they finally have their happy ever after a
second time around?

https://mybook.to/B0BYD85WFH

Ellie White

Acknowledgements

As always, this book wouldn't have been possible if it weren't for my family and the support and patience they have when I'm on a deadline.

And a huge thank you to my wonderful editor Aimee, for helping me get the best out of these characters and their story!

Finally, thank you to my hype team! Chels, Louise, Lyndsey and Melissa. Thank you for all of your words of encouragement and your hilarious voice messages!

About the Author

Ellie White was born and raised in Sunderland and is a proud Mackem! She lives in Houghton-Le-Spring with her husband and two young children. She supports Sunderland AFC and is a lover of chocolate, rom-coms, musicals and Formula One.

If you've enjoyed this book please leave a kind review on Amazon, Goodreads or Instagram, not forgetting to tag her! It doesn't have to be much, just a few words will do; it will make all the difference!

Follow her on Instagram @elliewhite_writes or search for her on Facebook, Twitter and Tik Tok to stay up to date with new releases!

Printed in Great Britain
by Amazon

33302469R00071